WANTED

Emma Jean, Heartbreak Queen

KAT ADDAMS

ISBN-13: 978-1-7364167-5-4

CHAPTER ONE

EMMA JEAN

M￼y mama had always taught me to wake before the Devil. She'd told me that once my feet hit the floor, I needed to live as if the Devil had woken, saying, *Oh no, she's up.*

But after my walk of shame back home from my latest adventure in California, I'd long since given up on rising earlier than the sun. Instead, I slept late, hidden in the safety of my bed, and let the Devil run loose in Gillibrook. Small-town gossip had to come from somewhere.

"Git up, Emma Jean!" My mother snatched the quilt from my bed. "Brother Roger needs a Sunday school teacher, and I volunteered you as tribute. Might as well be of some use around here. You ain't had a massage client in weeks." She marched toward the window and jerked open the blinds.

I shot up out of bed and rubbed my eyes. I hadn't even heard Peckerdoodle, our resident rooster, crow yet. But the strong scent of coffee and country ham down below signaled that our morning hospitality had already begun. We only had two brazen New Yorkers staying with us this week, and my grandmother, Mama Sue, was determined to convert their city-slicking life to a hoedown, one shot of whiskey in their coffee at a time. Not surprisingly, the guests happily obliged.

Much like my friend Josie, they'd traveled to Buck Off Ranch under false pretenses, claiming their soured love lives had turned them into bitter old cows. But I knew the truth. I sensed it in the way they slyly tugged down their tops and pursed their duck lips anytime the mailman dropped by or a Miller brother came to the barn to groom a horse. Those ladies had come here to peel the chaps off of a cowboy, no strings attached. Most of our guests did.

I had tried to explain that to my mama, but she only stuck her head in the dirt and ignored reality, refusing to believe in the magnetism of a tight pair of jeans and a cowboy hat. I couldn't blame her. Been there and done that. In my experience, a cowboy's rugged nature was code for selfish douche bag, and I was having none of it even if it was only for a quick roll in the hay. I could fiddle my diddle just as good as any cowboy *without* being left high and dry. For all the mouthwatering talk about cowboys I'd heard, the ones I had dated sure as hell didn't know the ropes when it came to filling my pleasure well.

But still, most of our guests weren't damaged women as much as they were horny huntresses on the cusp of a midlife crisis. They'd known mediocre all their lives by juggling a distant, workaholic husband and ungrateful kids who flew the coop quick as a whistle. These poor women were seeking out something *more*. I had been there and done that too —unsuccessfully.

"Mama! I can't go back to that church! You know the whole town will be there! I'm not ready to make my debut back in Gillibrook. Everyone will have my name on their lips the rest of the week." I balled the sheets in my fist and pulled them up under my chin, wrapping myself in protest.

On the rare days I left the ranch, I wore a redheaded disguise. I had ninety-nine problems, and small-town gossip wasn't one.

"Then, give 'em somethin' to talk about. Did you forget whose daughter you were?" She swirled on her heels and slammed my door shut.

Outside, Peckerdoodle crowed.

"How could I?" I moaned and rolled out of bed, shuffling my feet toward the bathroom to begin my exhausting skin care routine.

It hadn't been easy, being crowned pageant queen year after year when I lived in Gillibrook. The last time this town had seen the likes of me, I was young, wrinkle-free, hopeful, and *not* naive. Never naive. I knew my looks were a clever disguise by the way men and women regularly treated me. In one quick, innocent flutter of my thick lashes, they believed I was dumber than a sack of wet rocks. It was when they'd started to get to know me that they suddenly understood that they were playing with fire.

Like my mama had said, I was Abilene Presley's daughter. I knew when to hold 'em and when to fold 'em.

I stood in front of my mirror and pressed my fingertips to the corners of my jaw, dragging my skin upward and letting it fall back down with a sigh. At thirty, my skin was starting to lose the vibrant elasticity it'd had when I left this ranch. Now, my complexion had been dulled from years of disappointment. Disappointment in the men in my life, disappointment in my job prospects as a boss babe, and disappointment in myself. I named each fine line that began to show its wretched mark across my brow after my mistakes.

I leaned into the mirror and gasped, noticing a sliver of a wrinkle between my waxed brows.

"*West*," I spit out his name like a spoiled sunflower seed.

My eyes narrowed, deepening my new wrinkle until I realized I'd actively made it worse and smoothed my skin back in place. I slapped a heavy layer of moisturizer on my cheeks along with a handful of other products and cursed West Miller, my first heartbreak, for my latest flaw.

I couldn't avoid West Miller forever. These last few weeks, I'd successfully dodged him like a bullet. But in this small town, it was only a matter of time before I saw him. Everyone bumped elbows at some point. And that was the problem. I'd bumped the wrong elbow—or another body part—with his best friend ... more than once.

I snuck in through the back door of the church and headed to the children's nursery. Mama Sue had stayed behind to tend to our guests, but my mother, Abilene, strutted inside in her Sunday best. After all, she had a thing for the widowed Brother Roger, whether she wanted to admit it or not. She had invited him to Sunday supper numerous times, and this last time, he'd actually taken her up on the offer. I had known as soon as she pulled out her famous meaty Husband-Maker casserole from the oven that her dive back into the dating world had begun.

"Emma Jean! Why, I haven't seen you since you were runnin' through the pews in diapers," Gayle, a church elder, said. She clasped her hands under her chin and smiled. "Your mama said you'd be available to help. Lord knows, we need it. We have ten today, including Johnny P."

I took a step back, stifling a cough. Each time she shifted, I caught a whiff of heavy, outdated rose perfume and crusty, ancient makeup powder. She smelled as if she'd marinated in my grandmother's pocket.

"Yes, ma'am. I just got back into town recently." I jerked

my eyes from her wispy, spiderweb-like silver hair to the classroom full of hyper kids behind her. "Who is Johnny P.?"

"See that little boy over there, with the markers hanging from his nostrils?" She turned on her heels and tipped her chin to a small boy in the back.

He tore the markers from his nostrils and let out a roar, jumping on top of a chair and dancing.

"Oh." I wrung my hands behind my back and thought about the stiff drink I'd fix tonight.

"Well, come in. Don't be shy."

I stepped inside the door and shut it behind me, silencing the chorus of music echoing from the pulpit next door and locking myself in a room full of snot, dirty diapers, and Johnny P. Gayle walked to the corner of the room and stuck her hand inside a crib, shushing a baby with an old hymn I remembered from childhood. I closed my eyes for a split second, remembering my grandpa's voice trailing up through the pea patch. He'd sung the same tune on those sweltering summer mornings when I helped him harvest supper.

"Hey, lady! You can't sleep in here."

I felt a tug at my skirt and looked down at Johnny P. He folded his hands across his puffed-out chest and shot me an evil eye. I warded off my immediate reaction to back away and make the sign of the cross.

"I wasn't sleeping. I was remembering." The brief memory of my grandfather fled my thoughts as I faded back to the crowded room.

"No. I know what sleeping is. It's when you do this with your eyes," he said, shutting his eyes tight before opening them again. "You were sleeping. Fallin' asleep on the job. That's terrible. My daddy says only lazy, no-good sons of biscuit eaters do that."

"Johnny P.! We don't speak like that." Gayle gasped, covering her mouth with her palm.

"If I was sleeping, how do you explain me standing up?"

A group of little girls rushed by me, nearly knocking me down in a fit of giggles.

"You can do a lot of things when you're asleep. I know. I seen it. One time, Mama and Daddy were wrestlin' in bed when they were sleeping. I told them, 'Hey! No rough-housing inside.' That woke them up so fast. They were so ashamed they didn't have clothes on. I don't know what kind of dream they were having. Maybe pretending they were Adam and Eve before that rotten apple got in the way and spoiled everything. Now, we have lice, broccoli, and little sisters." He scuffed his tiny boot across the floor and ran away, chasing the group of girls and leaving me behind with flaming cheeks.

The door swung open, knocking against the wall.

"Party's here!" West jumped into the room with a dramatic flair, erupting the room in kiddie chaos.

I took a deep breath and sank my shoulders, realizing my time in church today was only a blip in my heavy penance. There wasn't any other explanation for the Karma I'd reaped since this morning. God saw fit to skin my hide, one minor disaster at a time.

"What are you doing here?" I rocked back on my heels and stood my ground as the crowd of children gathered around West, jumping up and down.

Johnny P. somersaulted and yelled, "Parkour," before landing at West's boots.

West fought his way through the munchkins and sidled up beside me with his trademark smirk.

My thoughts filtered back to the first time I'd met him. He'd worn a pair of dark blue jeans so tight that they looked as if he'd painted them on his rigid, muscled thighs. I could hardly tear my eyes from his tall, rawboned figure. But when I finally built the nerve to meet his gaze, his dove-gray eyes lassoed me to him for the rest of my high school days. Almost. That had been before our hellacious breakup senior year and before I knew what a turd muffin he could really be.

"I'm here to get my son," he said, scooping up Johnny P. in his arms.

I stumbled backward into a table, sending a box of crayons rolling to the ground. I dropped to the floor, frantically picking them up to hide my shocked expression. My mind spun with questions barreling through my thoughts like a bag of hammers, knocking my muddied brain this way and that.

Who is Johnny P.'s mom?

Did West get married?

Why didn't anyone tell me?

West set the boy down and stooped to help.

"Just kidding. That kid ain't mine." He laughed, exposing a row of stark white teeth against his bronzed jaw. I wondered if he'd ever moisturized his sun-drenched skin, but the faint smile lines creeping into the corners of his eyes told me he was still just as human as me. "You should have seen your face!"

I rose back up in a snap. He matched my energy, standing up and towering over me.

"Could have fooled me. If I pegged any unruly kid as yours …" I lowered my voice and looked out of the side of my view to make sure no one was listening. They weren't.

The children lost interest in us and began crawling all over Gayle as soon as she pulled out a box of cookies.

"Time for communion!" she said in a singsong voice.

I cut my eyes back to West, who stood, waiting for me to finish. A shadow of a beard crept along his jawline, leading to two half-parted full lips and a chin set with a defiant, stubborn streak. My lips tingled as I remembered his rough kisses and the way he'd threaded his fingers through my hair, pushing the back of my head into him with a firm, impatient grip.

"I … I …" I stammered.

"You were telling me which one of these kids was mine."

"Oh. Yeah. Which one is it again?" I casually waved a tendril of hair away from my damp brow.

He took a step closer toward me, filling my space with his familiar cedarwood scent. All of the Miller brothers carried the same raw, rugged aroma from years spent working in their barn and riding the land. But West's essence held a hint of provocative power that drugged me into a frustrating state of confusion. I liked it, but I hated it all the same.

"None." His mouth clamped shut.

"Oh." I let out a long breath I hadn't realized I'd been holding.

"I'm not married, and I don't have any kids. I guess you can say, I'm a heartbreaker, just like you."

"Can we not start this here?" I said, feeling Gayle's judgment on my back.

I glanced over my shoulder and met her eyes. She looked away and continued passing out cookies to eager, sticky little hands.

"And when do you propose we start it, Emma?" he asked.

"Never. I don't owe you an explanation for anything. Besides, what happened between us was over a decade ago. We were kids, fresh out of high school, for heaven's sake! I'd have thought a tough guy like you would have let it go already."

"Oh, I let it go all right." He jammed his hands in his pockets and rocked back on his boots. "I'm just wondering how long it's going to take you to run again."

"What's that mean?" I asked.

Gayle cleared her throat, commanding our attention. "Little ears."

"That's what my daddy says when Mama says the S-word. One time, she dropped a hot pan on her foot. She said the S-word eight times. I counted!" Johnny P. stuck his hand in the air, counting with his fingers.

I uncurled my fists and turned away from West to sit at the children's table. A little girl sat alone in a corner seat, coloring a picture of a house. Beside it, one tall stick figure and a smaller one stood on a block of scribbled green grass. A cat jumped through the air, curling itself in a crescent-moon shape in the background. The little girl leaned into the paper, sticking her tongue just over her bottom lip, and squinted in pure concentration.

"That's a pretty little house you got there, kiddo. Want to tell me about it? Is it yours?" I pulled out the tiny metal chair and dropped down beside her.

West shuffled toward the other end of the table and began to clean up the crumbs scattered across the top. The children chattered away as Gayle turned on an ancient tape recorder. Small voices rang out into the room, singing Bible songs.

"It's my house," the little girl said before writing her name at the bottom—*Katie*.

"Which window is to your room? Is it this one?" I pointed at a top window she'd colored yellow. "With the light on?"

"Yes, ma'am. I leave it on for Daddy. Mama used to always leave the porch light on for him because he worked late. But he doesn't come home anymore, and she turned it off. But I keep mine on for him. Shh. Don't tell her. I don't like sleeping in the dark anyway." She picked her picture up and held it close to her face, studying it.

A flash of wild grief gripped me, enveloping me in a tense silence I couldn't find the words to break. Gayle and the other children began to dance.

"Katie is Gillibrook's next famous artist. Isn't that right, Katie?" West sauntered over and plucked the artwork from

9

Katie's hands. He held it up to the light and beamed. "This one's it, Katie-Roo! This is the one you need to enter into the competition."

"But what if I lose, Mr. West?" She wrung her ink-stained hands in her lap.

"If you lose, it's not the end of the world. You just get back up and try again. It's called experience. You don't lose. You gain experience. You're winning just by having the ba— grit to put yourself out there. Isn't that right, Emma? You know, Emma Jean used to enter competitions too. I bet she could teach you a thing or two." His calm demeanor softened, lifting the mood and weakening my very much rational defenses.

I'd never had anyone tell me there was another option other than winning. My mother had taught me to play to win, aim to kill, and if I lost, I'd failed. Second chances weren't for strong women like us. We didn't get them, and we didn't dish them out. We switched gears and kept pushing forward, never repeating the same mistake or wallowing in weakness.

"You're going to the Weller County Fair, Miss Emma? Are you drawing too? Can you come see my picture? I don't think I'll win the blue ribbon. Do you have any blue ribbons? Or trophies? Can you show me?" Katie swung her legs back and forth under her seat and sat on her fidgeting hands. A hopeful glint beamed in her eyes.

Her rush of words, coupled with West's heartfelt conversation, threw me into a deep state of confusion. I hesitated, exchanging glances with West, who watched my bafflement with a smug delight he reserved for only me.

"I've won pageants. They're a little different." I gave a dismissive wave.

Katie's face brightened. "You're a beauty queen?"

"Gillibrook's finest. She never lost a competition she entered."

His smirk turned into a boyishly affectionate grin, and I knew he remembered the first time he had taken me to the pageant. My memories of the day were still pure and clear.

We had been flirty and friendly toward each other all summer long, but he was with Missy, and I was with Jake. When I got rid of Jake, West didn't take the hint. He still clung to Missy. But after Missy decided to expand her horizons—and by expand her horizons, I meant, spread her legs for every boy this side of the mountain—West was left all by his lonesome, single and on the prowl. But by that time, I had David in my back pocket.

We played this cat-and-mouse game for nearly a year before we both found ourselves single at the same time. That was the day he took me to the pageant. After I won my sash and crown, he scooped me in his arms and gave me a long-awaited smooch I'd never forget. He'd tasted like cotton candy and soda with a hint of precious teenage dream.

My cheeks burned at the memory. There wasn't any going back to those good ol' days without responsibility and baggage.

"Emma Jean?" he asked, my name rolling off his tongue and sending a tingle down the nape of my neck.

I pulled myself from my thoughts and back into the conversation, lifting my gaze to his. His gray eyes bore down into mine, flicking my desire for him back to life.

"I won a few. But I'm afraid I can't help you with art." I rose from my chair and told Gayle I wasn't feeling well before leaving in a hurry, apologizing to everyone in a jumble of words.

I hoped God didn't count this one against me too. I would have made it to the end of Sunday school if it wasn't for

West. Hell, I could sit next to the Devil himself and play it cool.

But West … he understood me as no one else could. He easily peeled my layers back, like he could see right through to my soul. I attributed his skill to the hardships he'd faced in his own life. But no matter because I didn't like to be seen like that, all naked and vulnerable. I fought like hell not to expose anything below my meticulously crafted surface.

One peek at my self-sabotaging soul, and my boyfriends would light a sage stick and smudge me out of their lives for good. That was why I always left first, leaving them in my dust, one heartbreak at a time. I couldn't suffer any more losses in my life. Every man I'd ever known disappeared without a fair warning.

Like my mama said, I always had to be one step ahead in the race.

I didn't know what kind of race I was competing in anymore, but just like in my old pageant days, I played to win. When it came to men, I didn't guard my fragile heart by only staying one step ahead. I nitpicked their flaws until I had an excuse to leave, and then I sprinted out of the race entirely.

CHAPTER TWO

WEST

I pulled my Jeep up the long gravel drive, passing by my brothers' cabins. Memphis and his motorcycle, as usual, weren't anywhere to be seen. Sawyer had stayed at church with my parents, and Tripp and Josie were outside, working on Josie's big yellow bus. I stepped on the gas pedal and swerved right, skidding up Tripp's drive. Clouds of dust plumed behind me. It hadn't rained in ages.

"I thought you were working Sunday school today," Tripp called out as soon as I parked and opened my door.

"I already did. Church has been over for an hour. Where you been?" I dug my good boots into the dusty gravel and walked toward the front of the bus.

Josie stood on a step stool, hovering above the open front hood.

"My head's been in this damn bus all morning. Thing is making a sound like it's about to dismantle itself soon as she hits the highway." Tripp wiped his face on a rag and slung it over his shoulder.

"Did I hear him say you taught Sunday school?" Josie hopped off the stool and smiled. She wore her hair in two long braids trailing down her shoulders from beneath a trucker hat that read *Bookin' it*.

"Yep. Not every Sunday, but some Sundays. I'm racking up all the good Karma I can to make up for"—I rubbed the scruff of my jaw and tried my best to hide a mischievous smile—"all the shit I used to do."

"Still do!" Tripp shouted. His voice echoed off the engine, vibrating the metal with his low drawl.

I looked past Josie at a butterfly flitting among the wildflowers. Their blossoms had faded and wilted from the late summer heatwave.

"I've heard the stories. Seems like you'd better show up to church every morning, noon, and night." Josie wiped her hands down her jean shorts and burst into laughter. "Aren't you the one who told that lady from Weller that you were building a seesaw for an orphanage down in New Mexico? You had to measure the bounce in it or something or other? Somehow, she ended up bouncing on you."

"What the heck kind of stories you telling your girlfriend there, Tripp?" Drops of moisture beaded across my brow from the sun—and my shame.

"Did I lie?" He jerked his head up from the engine and shifted from one foot to the other, grinning. He'd been wearing the same goofy grin since Josie had moved to Gillibrook.

My cheeks ached, just from me looking at it.

"First of all, yes, that was a lie. I was making a seesaw for grown-ups. The orphanage is another story entirely. You ever been to one of those breweries that's also a playground for adults? They got swings, volleyball courts, slides, and all that." I turned to Josie.

She shook her head.

"Anyway, I have. Folks from all over get drunk and let their inner kid out. But I saw a seesaw there. So, I was going to build one for adults—and I did. Sawyer and I seesawed every day for a week to try to get that thing as bouncy as it needed to be. It only landed with a thud and an unpleasant zap to our back ends. But then I lost interest, and Dad needed me for a cattle auction in Texas. The rest is history. Still got the seesaw in my backyard though."

"What about the girl?" she asked.

"Yeah, course she bounced on my dick. Pardon my language. But that had nothing to do with the seesaw or the orphanage … which I donated a full paycheck to, by the way. You know, Karma and all."

"I can't believe you and Sawyer played on a damn seesaw. Meanwhile, I was building chicken coops and breaking broncos." Tripp wiped his brow with the rag and shook his head before diving back into the bus's hood.

"It's still in your backyard, you say?" Josie made a steeple with her fingers, pressing the tips to her lips. Her face split into a wide grin, mirroring Tripp's lovesick expression.

I was happy for my brother. I really was. If two knuckle-heads were ever meant for each other, it was these two quirky lovebirds. But day after day, my brothers had something amazing going for them. Tripp had Josie, Memphis had his freedom, and Sawyer had anything he wanted because he was the spoiled baby of the family. And I … I had a damn oversize seesaw in my backyard and a bed full of just about every woman I could ever want. The problem was, I didn't want any of them.

"Yeah, it's back there," I muttered, rolling up my sleeves and walking toward my brother. I spread my palms on the rim of the hood and leaned in, inspecting the ancient engine.

Behind me, Josie disappeared inside Tripp's cabin.

"Can you describe the sound it's making?" I asked, brushing my palm over the bus's hot metal heart.

Oscar, Gillibrook's most trusted mechanic, had restored Josie's engine right after she arrived. With his skills, this bus should have been able to run smoothly for at least another five years.

"It's like a loud clinking. I gotta fix it before this weekend. She's setting up at the farmers market with Emma Jean on Saturday."

"Emma Jean?" I jerked my head up, nearly knocking it on the hood's underside.

"Yeah. Why? You still ... got the feels for her or something? Have you two rekindled your dramatic high school romance?" he asked, wiggling his brow and wiping his forearm across the sweat clinging to his upper lip.

"I've only seen her three times since she's been back."

"What? She's been back for months! How's that possible? Josie sees her most days, even working the library."

"I guess she's hiding out from me. Surprised she hasn't left yet."

"Why would she do that?"

"She's always running." I shrugged and forced a smile.

"I think she's here for good. I guess some guy broke her heart back in Cali. Apparently, he hurt her pretty bad," he said, leaning into me and lowering his voice.

"Speaking of Karma," I replied with heavy irony.

"Listen, if you're still upset about what happened back in high school, don't forget, that was over ten years ago. Both of y'all have grown up, and we all do dumb shit as teenagers. Besides, you can't exactly be mad about that. I keep telling you, y'all were broken up. She was fair game."

"But not with my best friend!" My nostrils flared.

"Like I said, we all do dumb shit when we're full of teen hormones. I know you did—you still do. I'm just saying. I think you and she should settle the dust. I heard she's still a blast to hang out with. Josie took her to Weller last weekend for a crawfish boil. She said Emma had all the men eatin' out of her hand! Literally. She sucked the heads off those mudbugs and fed them to a group visiting from Jackson Hole. Corporate clients. You know her type."

My mind whirled with visions of Emma Jean sucking the head off of anything. When we'd dated, she never even let me get past second base. The most play I'd gotten from her puckered little mouth or her soft, manicured hands was, respectively, a kiss on the lips and eight pumps to my jimmy before I blew my inexperienced teenage top.

"What're you boys going on about? Did I hear something about a crawfish-fest? Is there another one?" Josie popped up behind us with two iced teas sweating on a tray.

I jumped at the sound of her voice.

"Nah. I was just telling him about Emma Jean and you wooing the rich and famous in Jackson Hole."

"She's a firecracker, that one! Soon as she walked into that big white tent, every man there turned to watch her pass. She strutted down the aisle like this." Josie set the tray of drinks down on a nearby lawn chair and wiggled her hips, kicking up dust like a bull about to charge.

I tilted my brow. Beside me, Tripp licked his lips and undressed his girlfriend with his eyes.

"Well, not exactly like that. Durn. I thought I could nail it, but it's harder than I thought!" She waved a dismissive hand in the air and handed Tripp and me our drinks.

"Thank you." I dipped my head in thanks and peered back over the rim of the hood. "What did you say the noise sounded like again?"

"Clink-clunk, clink, clink-clunkety-clinky-clunk-clink," Tripp answered before taking a long sip of tea and sighing.

"Like a wrench being tossed around in there?" I asked.

"Yeah! Exactly like that! How did you know?" Josie bounced on her heels.

I stuck my hand inside the hood and pulled out a wrench. "Because there's a wrench bouncing around in here."

Tripp tugged at his collar. "Ooh-wee. Look at that! Must have been hiding underneath the … doomabobber."

I lowered my voice and spoke to him out of the side of my mouth. "It was right in front of your face, dipshit."

"You know I don't know anything about cars, just cattle. And plants and stuff. Survival. Not mechanics," he said to me, barely above a whisper.

"Yep. That was hidden deep in there! Glad you got me to spot it. My eagle eyes don't let much pass," I said a little too loudly, making sure Josie heard.

I tossed the wrench on the ground beside me.

"Well, would ya look at that? I guess old man Oscar must have left it in there all this time. Maybe I shook it up when I hit that weird lady last week. Poor woman had bolted out in front of me like she was running from something awful. And then she just vanished into thin air. If Emma Jean hadn't been with me, I'd have thought I imagined it. I still can't make heads or tails of it." Josie stooped to pick up the wrench and held it to her face, inspecting it.

"Tripp told me about that. Maybe she just ran off quicker than you two got your bearings. Anyway, he mentioned you and Emma were working the farmers market this weekend. That's pretty important. What're you selling?"

"Oh, well, I sell old, donated books to raise money for the bus. I'm hoping by next summer, I can hire some help at the library and take the summer off to the Appalachians. Some of those smaller communities could use my services, and I need to get back to see my parents at some point, I reckon. I think Emma Jean just volunteered to help me out because she wants to get out of the house. She's been working hard at Buck Off and needs the break. I feel like she's finally coming around to making her debut back in Gillibrook. She's had to … work up to it."

The thought of Emma Jean doing manual labor curled my toes. On the one hand, I wanted to see her sweating underneath the hot sun, caked in mud and decorated with last season's straw caught in her bouncy, ringlet curls. But, on the other hand, I wanted to see her typing away in some fancy office in the city, living the life she used to dream about.

My mind jerked back to the memory of her in Kyle's arms. He'd kissed her behind the bleachers homecoming night, shortly after we broke up for the fifth and final time. I didn't let either Kyle or Emma know I knew about their secret rendezvous until she came to school one morning with a peachy swatch of makeup smeared across her collar, masking a string of hickeys. Emma Jean had been avoiding me ever since.

"I bet," I ground out the words between my teeth and neglected to mention that she had shown her face earlier in Sunday school. "Maybe I'll see you two there. I need to pick up a few things anyway. Glad your bus is okay!" I turned to leave and jogged toward my Jeep.

"Thanks for fixing it!" Josie called out.

"Yeah! Thanks for finding that wrench! I knew that had to be it! Just couldn't find the sucker!" Tripp threaded a hand through his hair before waving good-bye.

I pulled out of their driveway and headed to my cabin.

Bitter jealousy stirred below my surface, not for the way Emma had sauntered back into Gillibrook and expected things to be the same and not even for the way she never apologized for rolling in the hay with my then best friend,

Kyle. But the envy that bubbled up inside my chest lingered because I knew the second she roped another cowboy to play with, she'd run away again, and my only chance to reignite the chemistry we'd once shared would ride off into the sunset with her.

I WOKE UP, sinking into the crevices of my old couch. The time on the clock in the kitchen read that it was just past midnight, and the sound of raucous laughter outside my back door had rudely woken me from a peaceful and comfortable slumber. I rubbed my eyes and rolled off the couch I chose to sleep on most nights.

When I snoozed on my worn-in cushions, I slept within walking distance of the fridge, the TV, and my trusty massage chair I'd named Buffy. I had bought her last year on a Black Friday sale. The damn thing had nearly cost me two paychecks, but she was worth every. Single. Penny. After a long day of breaking in a wayward horse or catching, roping, and branding cattle, my thirty-year-old body ached for a rough, deep massage.

Other than the massage room at Buck Off Ranch, Gilli-brook didn't have a real spa experience. I'd had to travel all the way across Mount Odina to get my kinks worked out— and that was in all the ways. Women around my small town were few and far between, but Weller was the pot of gold at the end of a batshit-crazy rainbow. I could take my pick of any of those broads and know I was in for a good time. At least, I suspected that when I booked a massage—before I bought Buffy.

I'd seen enough porn to know about happy endings. One quick look at the massage studio's website showed a row of beautiful, beaming women, ready to tickle their soft palms over my backside. The business's gushing reviews were all written by men who'd said they had enjoyed the special treatment and how the massage therapists had gone above and beyond to create a *pleasing* experience. In my neck of the woods, *special treatment, going above and beyond,* and *pleasing experience* meant these dudes had received an expert hand job with no strings attached and then skedaddled on their merry way.

So, naturally, after I booked my appointment, I prepared myself for a good ol' rub and tug and hightailed it to Weller. I figured I would pull all of my winning moves and entice whatever bombshell lubed me up to yank my oiled crank. I would begin by only speaking in the firm, deep, tantalizing voice women loved. One slip of my famous breathy growl, and my flings wiggled right out of their lacy drawers.

But I didn't want to push any buttons that didn't want pushing. I wasn't an asshole. Instead, I put some feelers out, and if she took the bait, I would continue flirting, using my biggest asset—my cock. I'd not so subtly drape the sheet over my well-endowed member, letting him peek out from time to time each time she rolled me over. *Oopsie!* The python had a mind of its own.

When I finally built enough anticipation, I walked into the massage studio with my foolproof plan. I eagerly stripped down to my birthday suit and hopped atop the table, ready to go. As with all Miller luck, things quickly turned sour when the door opened, and Jack, my eighty-two-year-old massage therapist, introduced himself and began to work my neck with callous hands that smelled like rancid turnips. My dick shriveled faster than a forgotten hot dog left cooking in the microwave.

Shortly after that terrible incident, I'd given up my massage fantasy and purchased Buffy. She never let me down.

I flicked my eyes toward my massage chair and wondered if I was too tired to tug while she rubbed. Another fit of laughter burst through my cracked window, drifting inside and waking me from my daze.

"What the fuck is this racket?" I peered out into the dark.

Josie and Tripp were skyrocketing back and forth atop the seesaw. Her hair flew up with each plop on her rear when Tripp dug his heels into the ground and pushed. They'd both snuck over, barefoot and half-dressed. A nearly empty six-pack of beer lay at my brother's feet.

"Lightweight," I muttered and turned to leave them alone.

I couldn't fault them two goofuses for letting loose. When Josie had arrived to stay in Gillibrook for good, it was the first time my brother had been truly happy since his twin had passed. Josie hadn't shown up as only his savior, but she had become all of the Miller family's hero too. Her light in Tripp's life was a sigh of relief in ours.

More joy for them was less worry for me. As the eldest brother, it fell on me to lead my siblings forward in their lives. But Tripp ... I'd honestly believed his traumatic experience had damaged him for good. Just last summer, after a brutal argument, I'd almost given up on pushing him back into the world entirely. Now, I could kick myself for even entertaining the idea even though I hadn't been the one to ultimately coax him from his shell. I didn't give two shits how he'd learned to live again as long as he did. Hell, I hoped they seesawed all night long.

I shook my head and smiled before opening the fridge and grabbing the milk carton. I took a long swig straight from it, emptying it down my gullet. A schedule for the Weller County Fair hung loosely on my fridge under an ancient magnet from my parents' Niagara Falls honeymoon. I tossed my milk jug in the trash and plucked the schedule from the fridge, holding it up to my eyes to study it in the dim light.

I'd planned on loading up the wagon and taking my brother Sawyer so that he could compete in the bull-riding championship. But after my parents received a phone call from the fair committee, saying they needed our horses for some kind of arena show, my mother had volunteered both Tripp and me to drag the horse trailer out there and stay all damn day long.

I flipped the paper over and skimmed through the local contests.

Desserts, barbecue, and fried foods.

Moonshine.

Jerky tasting.

Tractor pull.

Archery.

Cornhole.

Pig mud wrestling.

Fowl rodeo.

Art.

Cat show.

Dog show.

Cow costumes.

Weller 5K.

County fair queen pageant.

Blue Ribbon Championship games.

And more ...

I began reading aloud through the sub-contests and toying with the idea of making Tripp join me in a few to pass the time. *"To claim the Blue Ribbon Championship, you must win first place in at least three events, including one teamwork event. Winner takes home bragging rights, a Weller County trophy from Bob's Metals, free ice cream at Lou's all summer long, a bag of swag, and a one-night stay with a massage at Buck Off Ranch."* I lowered the brochure. "Fuck. Buck Off Ranch?"

I hung the schedule back on the fridge and inhaled a deep breath. If I couldn't get Emma Jean to come to me, I would have to go to her. There would be no escaping our much-needed *clear the air* conversation in her own home. After all, once I cleared this damn stifling air, maybe we could pick up where we'd left off. We could give each other the second chance we both deserved even if I had to act like her and break a few hearts along the way.

I shuffled back to the couch amid a chorus of giggles coming from outside. A stab of guilt buried itself deep inside my chest as I plopped down on the cushions and closed my eyes. I had to slowly back off Katie's mom—sweet Marie, a widow—in the most honest way possible. I'd taken her on a handful of dates, and our relationship had slowly been progressing until Emma Jean came back. Emma's arrival had sparked a magnetic vitality in my bones that I hadn't felt since she'd left.

I didn't care if Emma and I had been young and dumb back then and clueless about true love and all it entailed. The lurch of excitement that still crossed my thoughts anytime her name popped into my mind couldn't be replicated by anyone else. Even after all this time. Believe me, I'd tried. I'd chased the high of my high school sweetheart for years, only coming close once with a woman from Emma Jean's own ranch—go figure. But that didn't last. She'd run too.

I couldn't give myself to Marie and Katie and commit to a lifetime of settling when the one woman who took my breath away still lingered around the edges of my mind, even after she'd shattered my heart into a million prickled splinters. There wasn't anyone else who allured me with an aching desire and an all-around passionate love that refused to release me from its iron grip.

It had always been Emma, and it would always be Emma. She could run all she wanted, but I would never stop chasing her. Instead, I'd win this damn blue ribbon; finally snag a chance to have a serious, private conversation with Emma; and give her a reason to stay.

CHAPTER THREE

EMMA JEAN

I HOPPED OFF OF JOSIE'S BUS AND BEGAN HELPING HER UNPACK boxes of books to set them out for display on her small folding table. We were the last vendor to arrive at the bustling Gillibrook farmers market. Many farmers had unpacked their harvest at sunrise, setting out crates of shining cucumbers and peppers, loaded trays of tomatoes, and piles of corn, still wrapped in silken husks.

"I can't believe people around here get started so early!" Josie said, picking through a box of books and propping the best-looking covers on the table. She stashed the other boxes on the ground with a sign marking every book two dollars or three for five bucks.

"Well, it's a farmers market. You know, farmers work from dawn until dusk." I brushed my hair from my face and wound it through a ponytail holder before placing my hands on the back of my hips and stretching my spine.

The scent of root vegetables and cured meats wafted from the table beside us, causing my stomach to lurch into a furious growl. I peered down the rows of tables and searched for a quick bite of breakfast. Toward the end of the market was a giant sign that read *Mrs. B's Bakeshop*. A handful of people gathered around the vendor, blocking my view of whatever pastries lay in the display cases. But to get to Mrs. B's, I would need to pass half of everyone who had attended my old high school, and I wasn't in the mood to fake smile at Bobby Sue or Billy Jean—especially after I'd heard about their notorious thrill for small-town gossip.

"What's that look in your eyes?" Josie asked, pausing to stand next to me and follow my gaze.

"I was just thinking about how hungry I am. But if I want to eat, I'll have to do the walk of shame the entire length of this damn farmers market. Everyone's going to know I'm back, which means I failed in the big city and came crawling home to roost." I ran my palm down my bright yellow sundress and set my jaw.

"I can go get us breakfast. I'm starving! Do they have jelly doughnuts around here anywhere?" she asked.

"You and your jelly doughnuts." I shook my head. "I'll get us breakfast. This is something I have to do. I can't hide any longer. It's about time Gillibrook knows I'm back. They'll all speculate and talk, but it'll die down eventually, and I'll become old news."

"I got your back. If anyone calls you a varmint or nincompoop, I can wrestle, you know." She cracked her knuckles and grinned.

"Is that another story from one of your books, or are you for real?"

"Story. But that's our little secret. Go sashay those hips down that aisle and show them the queen is back!" She leaned against the bus and opened the doors, signaling for customers to come inside and browse her mobile library.

Behind us, a train whistled in the distance, drowning out

the sound of a local bluegrass band set up in the center of the market. My feet grew light as I took my first step out into the judgmental public eye. I took a deep breath and adjusted my smile, focusing directly ahead of me, but the lure of the tables surrounding the market was too distracting. Before I knew it, I'd stopped in front of a table overflowing with buckets of fresh flowers. Their petaled heads swayed in the gusty breeze drifting through the tents.

"Good morning, miss. How can I help you today?" A woman stepped up from behind the table. She wore a heavy-handed hot-pink blush across her cheeks and a saucy grin that barely masked a chipped front tooth. Her entire right arm was decorated with a skull and rose tattoos.

"Evelyn?" I raised my eyebrow a fraction.

"Oh my word!" Evelyn covered her mouth with her hand before lowering it to her side. "Emma Jean Presley! When did you get back?"

"Eh, not long ago."

"What brings you back to this shithole? Are you staying awhile? You at Buck Off?" she asked, throwing her lengthy black dreadlocks behind her back.

If there was ever anyone in my high school class who had been the subject of more rumors than me, it was Evelyn. The poor girl's eccentric demeanor scared off everyone—boys included. But deep down, I knew that didn't matter because Evelyn didn't care about boys.

"I'm not sure how long I'm staying, but yes, I'm with my mom for a bit." Heat pooled inside my chest, twisting my nerves until I could figure out an escape.

"Here, babe." A thin-lipped woman rose from under a table and set out a tray of herbal tinctures before dipping back down to grab another.

"That's Vanessa, my wife. And over there"—she tilted her

head to two young children running through the booths—
"those are ours."

"What a beautiful family! And you grow all of these
flowers here in Gillibrook? Did you buy a farm or something?" I quickly changed the subject to her business.

As much as I was ready to make my debut back in my
small town, I hadn't prepared myself for any questions. Truth
be told, I didn't have an answer for any of them, and lies
weren't my thing.

"Vanessa's family owned a farm that she inherited a few
years back. They had sold potatoes, but we wanted to try
something new, fresh, artistic. Check these out." She picked a
pack of herbs from the tray and handed it to me.

"What's this?" I turned it over in my hand and scanned
the label.

"They're used for all sorts of things. But this one is good
for warding off the evil eye and … assholes, I like to say." She
winked and leaned forward, spreading her hands on the
table. "All yours. My treat."

"But what makes you think I need it?" I held the pack up
to my nose and inhaled. The scent of leafy greens and spice
clung to the thin fabric wrapping.

"Because you're in Gillibrook. If anyone knows how
outsiders are treated, it's me."

"But I'm not an outsider." I shifted my weight on my feet
and curled the herbs in my palm.

"You've been gone a long time. You're an outsider now. I
hate to say it, but nothing much has changed. And the last
time you were here, you caused quite a ruckus in our little
town. These people remember. They don't forget anything,"
she said, rolling her eyes.

"Shit. I knew people couldn't let bygones be bygones." I
stepped closer to the table, letting a woman with armloads of

plastic bags squeeze by me. She bumped into my back, knocking my hips against the corner of the table.

"They don't mean any harm. They're mostly just curious. Found that out after I came out. But still, gotta keep your guard up." She opened her arm wide, letting one of her two children slide in beside her before wrapping the little girl snugly against her. Her other child was still running circles between the aisles.

The bluegrass band quieted and told the crowd they were taking a quick break.

"You sound like my mama." I lowered my voice. My throat ached with exhausted defeat already.

"Because I'm a mama. It's good advice." Evelyn narrowed her eyes and studied my face, no doubt wondering if I had any children of my own.

"You're pretty," Evelyn's daughter said, stuffing her hand in a plastic bag and pulling out a peach before handing it to me. "For you."

I grabbed the fuzzy peach in my free hand, brushing off the dusty bit of dirt clinging to it. "Well, thank you! Thank you both. I didn't mean to stop by and load up on goodies like this. Let me buy some flowers. I'll take a handmade bouquet for my friend Josie. She's in that big yellow school bus down there. You should stop by and check it out," I said quickly and pulled a wad of cash out of the front pocket of my dress, setting down a twenty. "You can keep the change. I completely forgot she's waiting on me to bring back breakfast."

Evelyn plucked a variety of golden sunflowers, flecked with an inky-black pattern, from buckets and tied them together with string. "Here you go. These are new this summer. We had to order them after Little Bit here saw they were called the Princess Penelope variety. No idea why, but whatever makes my kids happy." She nudged her daughter on the shoulder.

The little girl beamed back up at her mom.

"They're beautiful. Thanks again!" I slipped the herbal pack in my pocket and grabbed the flowers before turning to leave.

I had felt the eyes of the entire market watching our exchange. I hoped they had seen my herbal talisman and kept their distance for the rest of my visit.

I tipped my chin up and brought the peach to my lips, inhaling its sweet scent before taking a bite and strolling through the rest of the booths, heavily relying on my evil-eye voodoo to ward off asshats. Sticky peach juice slid down my arm, catching on the inside of my elbow. I wiped my arm across my dress and carried on like a local country girl and not the cultured, stiff-laced city doll the citizens had rumored me to be.

I passed by decorated tablecloths stacked high with quilts; a booth full of large, round pungent cheese wheels; and rows upon rows of ripening berries before I neared Mrs. B's. I tossed my peach pit in a nearby trash can and took my time, wandering the market and nodding to old friends without making eye contact or pausing to chat. But the mouthwatering scent of spice stopped me in my tracks, leaving me standing as vulnerable as a gazelle amid a pack of lions. I stuck my nose in the air, closed my eyes, and inhaled before moaning. I couldn't help it. The scent reminded me of Christmas memories, wrapped in a sugar-coated dessert. I had to have it.

"What's that smell?" I whispered to myself before opening my eyes again.

"Dee's Nuts," came a deep, rugged voice from behind me.

As if on cue, the band began playing again. The fiddler strummed his instrument with a sad *womp, womp, womp.*

31

I swirled on my heels and came face-to-face with West. He towered over me with the devilish smirk that lured in just about every lady he passed—myself included. I planted my heels firmly on the ground, bracing my boundaries against his hypnotic magnetism and cursing the evil-eye voodoo charm that hadn't worked.

"Excuse me?" I sputtered, bristling at his remark.

"Dee's ... Nuts." He pointed to a crowded booth piled high with greasy, waxed paper cones full of roasted nuts, stacked candy bars, and baskets of chocolates.

His gaze slid down my sticky chin to my exposed collar before settling on my breasts. My nipples tingled beneath the thin cotton fabric.

"Oh." I glowered at him and turned away, walking toward Dee's Nuts.

"Wait!" he called out after me.

My heart jolted, hammering against my rib cage like it could escape. I clutched the flowers to my chest and shoved my free hand in my pocket, squeezing the useless talisman Evelyn had given me. I picked up my pace until I made it to Dee's table, working my way in between two other customers grabbing their change and goodies.

"Dee! I'll take two pecan cones and two fudge bars, please!" West shoved himself beside me and threw his hand in the air, grabbing Dee's attention before I could politely place an order.

She lifted her head and parted her mouth in a wide grin, displaying a row of pearly-white teeth underneath two racy red lips. Her polka-dot dress hugged her hourglass curves like a '50s pinup, barely covering her overflowing cleavage. I glanced down at my simple sundress and wiped away a stray chicken feather that had somehow found its way to my hemline.

"I don't need you to buy me anything! If you think this

means I owe you, you're wrong!" I hissed as I turned toward West, my voice cutting like a knife through the short distance between us.

"I always thought if you had a chance to try Dee's Nuts, you'd love them." He looked at me with a tempting curve of his mouth.

I slowly inhaled, breathing in a mixture of his minty mouthwash and Dee's Nuts. Around us, women slowed as they passed, appreciatively glancing at his tall, chiseled features. I buckled, fighting back the urge to step into him even closer. He reached out his hand, sensing my confusion, but let it fall to his side before he touched me. My skin flushed crimson.

"Mr. West! Mr. West!" Katie ran up to West and jumped into his arms.

He picked her up and twirled before setting her back down.

"Sorry! I told her not to run off."

A woman—slightly younger than me with short, curled hair—jogged toward us, stopping next to West and hugging him. She had thin hips that tapered into long, straight legs and peach-tinted skin, dewy from the sun. Her arm brushed against his, sending the hairs on his forearm to stand on end. A deep blush rose from his collar.

"West, here's your order." Dee interrupted their exchange and handed him a paper bag from across the counter, slowly letting the bag go while lingering her fingers on his a moment too long.

Her pale-yellow hair fell around her shoulders like glowing fields of grain. She fluttered her thick lashes and grinned, illuminating her high cheekbones and youthful features. There wasn't a single line in her porcelain skin.

I shrank back, clutching the flowers against me even

harder. The woman next to West stared at Dee as she stared at West.

"You're the beauty queen!" Katie pointed at me and grinned.

"Honey! Don't point!" The woman swatted her daughter's hand away and tore her attention from Dee to me.

West pulled his wallet from his back pocket and slid a twenty-dollar bill toward Dee with a shaky hand. "Thanks! Keep the change."

Dee stuffed the money in her bra and winked before helping a customer behind her. The woman next to West dropped her gaze to Dee's perky, perfectly round apple bottom and blew a long breath out of her nose.

"Marie, this is my old friend Emma Jean. Emma Jean, this is Marie. And Katie's already met Emma from Sunday school." West left Dee's table and motioned us to follow, distancing himself from her flirty glances.

"Oh. You teach Sunday school?" Marie asked as we turned away from the crowded booth and toward an empty cramped space nearby.

She stepped back into West, raking her back against his chest. She tilted her head up to gaze into his eyes and quickly mumbled something I couldn't hear. He nodded with a taut jerk of his head.

"Not really. I just heard they were short-staffed one day and stumbled into the job. But it was just that once." I gave a dismissive wave but never took my eyes off West. *Why is he acting so strange?*

He thrust his jaw forward and pulled his lips into a thin, tight line. I could sense his stifling unease.

"She's going to the fair, Mama! She liked my art." Katie reached up and grabbed her mom's hand, tugging it.

"Is that right? Katie mentioned something about a beauty queen. Are you competing?" Marie asked me.

"No. I'm—" I started before West rudely interrupted me.

"Actually, that's what we were discussing. One of the Blue Ribbon Championship prizes is a night at Buck Off Ranch, complete with a massage. I was going to ask her about that because I've decided to compete for the grand prize. Might as well since Tripp and I will be stranded at the fairgrounds all day." He leaned back and smirked.

Whatever nervousness he'd held, standing between his girlfriend and me, evaporated with the thrill of his plans.

The blood drained from my face at the mention of a massage at my place. I hadn't had a client since I'd moved in, and West sure as hell wouldn't be the first on my table. I wrinkled my nose as the realization of his shenanigans washed over me. West was on a mission to discuss my fuckup with his best friend and wrestle the truth out of me one way or another. But opening up and exposing myself to the one man who still made my heart tick was a volatile danger I refused to entertain.

I stuck my hip out and cradled my bouquet in front of me like a true pageant queen. My expression sank into my reliable poker face. Mama would be so proud.

"I'm afraid I can't offer you any tips. You see, I'm also competing for the Blue Ribbon Championship, so I can freshen my skills. I heard they got ... prizes. And you know me. I love a good challenge," I said, fighting to maintain my curtness.

"Oh?" He tapped his finger to his chin and raised his brows half a fraction. "So, you *are* staying. You know, some of the events aren't for the faint of heart. They have pig mud wrestling and Fowl Rodeo. I didn't think you were into all that. I thought you were more *polished*."

"Who? Me? Nonsense." My tone grew heavy with sarcasm. "Just because I wear a crown doesn't mean I can't get down and dirty with the rest of the contestants. I do live on a ranch, you know. Buck Off is in my blood."

West pursed his lips and blew out a long-drawn-out breath.

"So, you're the one from Buck Off I keep hearing everyone talk about." Marie eyed me suspiciously.

Beside her, Katie stirred with impatience.

"I'm not sure what you mean by that. Tell me, what type of pathetic gossip are they saying?" I asked, puckering my lips in annoyance.

Marie hesitated, blinking back bafflement at my unwelcome frankness. West stared down at his boots.

"I didn't mean to come out snarky. It's just that this town has its nose everywhere it doesn't belong. Have you lived here long?" I asked.

"No. I moved here for my husband's job, but he passed about a year ago," she replied.

"I'm sorry to hear that." Guilt struck me in the gut. My anger evaporated as I recalled Katie's artwork and the light she'd left on for her dad. My stomach clenched tight, as I was unnerved by the sudden, dramatic change in the atmosphere.

"Thank you. West has stepped in and been a big help after the accident. He knew Brett. They were friends there for a bit."

She put her arm around Katie's shoulders and pulled her in close. The little girl eyed the bag of goodies dangling from West's hand.

I stole a glance at West's reaction to her confession, but he looked away from me and busied himself with examining the booths behind us.

"I'm so glad he's been a help. Listen, I'm sorry to dash off like this right after meeting you, but I'm working my friend Josie's bus, and I was only supposed to be gone long enough to pick up breakfast." I slowly backed away, straining against my fragile composure.

"Here, take the nuts," West called, holding out his hand.

I shook my head. "Give them to Katie and Marie. Josie wants pastries. I'll see you around!" I dashed off, disappearing into the crowd before anyone could stop me.

Up ahead, Josie squinted through her angular cat-eye glasses until I came into full view. Behind her stood an older woman, wrapped in a crocheted afghan, stooped over and rummaging through the boxes of books. Customers filed in and out of the bus with empty hands.

"Where're the doughnuts?" Josie asked. Loose tendrils of hair escaped her messy bun, clinging to her damp face.

I set the bouquet down on the table placed in front of the bus. "No time to eat. Sorry. I couldn't go back there. Something terrible has come up. I've got a situation."

"Oh no! What happened? Did someone say something? Do I need to show them these guns?" Josie rolled up her sleeves and flexed a pitiful muscle that looked like half a lump of coal attached to a broomstick.

"No, no. Not yet anyway. It's about the fair. I just decided to enter myself into a competition, competing against the last person I want to go up against so I can stop him from coming to Buck Off. My mom generously donated a stay at our ranch as the grand prize, and I'll be damned if that sucker sets foot in my quarters. I've got to sabotage the event or win ... or else."

"Who is it? Who's the man you're so worried about?"

"West."

"Tripp's brother?"

"Yes!"

"Why do you two hate each other so much? I thought high school sweethearts were supposed to harbor a long-lost love forever. At least, that's what my romance novels say. I couldn't tell you for sure. The closest I ever got to a boyfriend in high school was the doughnut baker I met every morning. He got a little flirty at times, but he was also seventy-four. Now that I think about it, that's pretty creepy." She covered her face with her hands and blew out a breath before shrugging. "Age gap."

"I don't hate West." I turned my head left and right and grabbed Josie's dainty wrist, tugging her behind the bus, where no curious ears lingered.

She yelped and followed behind me, glancing back at the customers lazily wandering around the boxes.

"Listen up because I hate telling this story, and I'm only saying it once. West and I were friends forever, but both of us were, for lack of better words, overwhelmed with flirty attention. He had girls flinging themselves at him, and I had guys flinging themselves at me. When we finally flung ourselves at each other, I got scared. We were the typical on-again, off-again boyfriend and girlfriend, and it was fine up until senior year. But I knew I wanted to spread my wings and get the hell out of Gillibrook right after graduation, and West wouldn't ever leave his family or his ranch, so we both knew it wouldn't work. Our opposite desires for our future put us at odds a lot."

"You two broke up, so you could both pursue your dreams? Nothing wrong with that." Josie folded her arms across her chest.

"Not exactly. I didn't get accepted to the school I'd wanted to go to, so I was stuck for a little while longer than I wanted to be in Gillibrook. But at that time, he and I had both decided to step back from each other and take a break because all we did was argue. Well, when he stepped back, his best friend, Kyle, stepped forward. He told me West was dating again and had the hots for my friend Becky. So, I figured all was fair in love and war, and I lost my virginity ... to Kyle. *Pure, raw, mouthwatering sex on a stick* Kyle."

Josie put a hand to her mouth and dropped her jaw before recovering. "Ouch. Is that what West is still mad about then? You were broken up though. I mean, I get that it was his best friend. That would sting like hell. But if you two weren't together, does that break some sort of code?"

"Not if he's out there, supposedly banging my friends too! Becky was captain of the cheer team that I was also on. Thankfully, when all this happened, school was nearly over. So, I didn't have to deal with her, and Kyle and West never spoke again after that either. They had been best friends since they were little, known around town as the incredible duo. It didn't take long for the entire town to blame me for breaking up the band. But when all this came about and my mom saw me crying in my room day and night, that shit really hit the fan." I scrubbed my palms down my face and wiped them on my dress.

"What fan? What shit?" Josie asked me in a rush of words. Her voice grew into a high pitch as she teetered on the edge of my tragic love story.

"My mom, Abilene, told me everything about her divorce from my dad. She'd always been hard on me, growing up, but I hadn't really known why or the full details of their split. But after she spilled the beans on my dad's affair, I decided to avoid that kind of drama and heartache forever."

I bit my lip and continued, "My dad left when I was young. My grandfather died when I was young. And West? Anytime we got in an argument, he would haul off for days without speaking to me. My track record with the opposite sex was shit. They all left. So, ever since then, I'd bail first before any man could leave me, except that asshat Tommy Pickins. He just disappeared completely off the face of the earth without ever contacting me again. See? Lesson learned. Again."

"Hold up. Let me get this straight." She rubbed her palms together. "You're afraid of living a life like your mom, so you put up walls?"

"Yes."

"Poor you and poor Abilene. I get it. My parents never had those issues, but I read about character wounds a lot, and, lady, you're a fine example of father abandonment. No offense."

"That's why my mom toughened me up. She saw what was coming when it came to boyfriends, so she scared me away from them entirely. I dated men left and right to maintain any sense of normalcy, but I always bailed before things got serious. It earned me even more of a bad reputation around here."

"People just don't know. They don't understand." She waved her hand in the air. "And frankly, it's none of their damn business. They haven't walked a mile in your shoes! You'll figure it out one day, once the right man sweeps you off your boots and into trust."

"Maybe. But that's small-town gossip for you. Anyway, this is all beside the point. The point is, I'm avoiding West because, for one, I don't need to explain banging his best friend since I'm pretty sure he banged my friend, too, and we had already broken up! And for two"—I lowered my voice and leaned against the bus—"I can avoid him, but I can't run from him. I want to run to him. The chemistry we shared in our short-lived relationship, I haven't found that since. You ever have an old injury that aches on a rainy day?"

Josie caressed her elbow and nodded.

"It's like that. Except West is my achy wound and every day is another storm. That's one delicious maelstrom I wouldn't be able to escape from." My voice wavered.

"Then, why escape from it? Why can't you two just sit down and talk like adults and let whatever happens happen? Maybe he's the one you can trust. Y'all were young back then, and the past is the past."

"Well, it looks like he has a girlfriend who needs him more than I do now. And also because I'm not planning on staying in Gillibrook much longer. Why put myself between them and their relationship and torture myself, knowing it wouldn't work out between West and me? This is the same predicament we debated on in high school."

"Girlfriend? I didn't know that. I'm surprised Tripp hasn't mentioned it." She adjusted her glasses and stuck out her bottom lip. "Where are you going when you leave Gillibrook?"

"Here. There. Wherever the storm takes me."

"Have you ever considered therapy?"

I threw my head back and let out a burst of laughter. "I think I'll pass on therapy. All I need is a good man and a good ear—not a cowboy and not a local. I know myself. I've just never found anything good enough worth settling for, is all."

"Mmhmm. I'd say, give West another chance, but I trust you know what's best for you. But I can be your ear whenever you need me. As far as the sausage-fest, you're out of luck here. The only bits I possess are Dee's Nuts. Did you get a chance to try them?" She pulled a package of nuts from her back pocket and jiggled them in the air.

"When did you get those?" I grabbed the bag and brought them to my nose, inhaling the spiced scent.

"A regular gave them to me. He mentioned her business is hopping down there and wanted to bring some by before she sold out."

I plucked a toasty almond from the bag and popped it in my mouth. The conflicting mixture of salty and sweet hit the back of my tongue. I savored the flavor, chewing on the memory of the way Dee had licked her lips while looking at West. I'd immediately grown jealous and confusingly turned on.

"Hello? Earth to Emma." Josie waved her hand in front of my face. "Give me those! If they make you drool like that, I need to try one." She grabbed the bag back from my hand and began to chomp.

"Sorry. I was just thinking about the competition," I lied, trying to calm my heated body.

"What's in it for you? Why do you want to win?" Josie tossed a nut in the air and opened her mouth to catch it. It fell to the ground and rolled underneath the bus. She tipped the bag up and shoveled a handful between her lips.

"Because my mom donated a night at Buck Off Ranch, complete with a massage, as the grand prize. If he wins, he gets to stay over at my place, and I have to be stuck in a tiny room, massaging him. So, I'll win it instead and avoid the whole damn situation."

My mind drifted back to fantasyland with a new, filthy kink I'd been aching to explore beneath my massage table.

Back in the city, I'd mostly massaged little old ladies and tired old men. But if I had the pleasure of running my palms down a cowboy with a rock-hard set of abs, open to more than just a rub, I'd slip under my table and yank the rooster, mastering complete control over him until he melted in my hands. I'd devour his nuts similar to how Josie had devoured Dee's—like a rabid, starved chipmunk—swallowing them nearly whole before licking my lips, satisfied.

"Wait. Since when did you learn massage therapy?" she asked between mouthfuls.

"I've always had a license. We just don't get many looking for that sort of thing here. I haven't had a client since I left the city. So, instead, I've had to work the ranch." I rolled my eyes.

"Maybe you can show me some moves!" Her eyes lit up, and for a moment, I wondered if we shared the same trail of thought. "But what if you don't win?"

"Well, let's just hope the winner is a tall, dark, and handsome man who isn't local and will leave first thing the next morning." I brushed my palms together and let myself fall into this thirst trap.

I hadn't been laid since last winter.

"Tall, dark, handsome. Sounds like West." She threw another nut in the air, this time catching it and nearly choking.

"Not West." I shook my head and fought the urge to entertain the idea of a no-strings-attached night with the one man who could still send a rush of heat between my thighs with just one look.

CHAPTER FOUR

WEST

I clicked my boots against my horse and picked up the pace, scanning fence posts for loose wire. Deep, rutted tracks from the tractor snaked through the dirt, marking where we'd cut the grass yesterday but stopped just short of the south pasture when it began to sprinkle.

This morning, I'd noticed Memphis's motorcycle parked under his carport, so I'd banged on his door and woken him up at the crack of dawn. My black-sheep brother would earn his keep, whether he liked it or not. He hadn't put up too much of a fight before roping his horse and meeting us in the fields after I told him our father would be joining us. If there was anything Memphis feared—and there wasn't much—it was my father's stern rebukes and disappointment.

"West, Tripp, you two ride over yonder past the creek. Check on Marley's side. Memphis and I'll finish up here," my dad said, yelling over Sawyer approaching on the rumbling tractor in the distance.

I patted my horse's warm flank and told it, *"Giddyup!"*

"What's all that about?" Tripp asked.

"I guess he wants a word with Memphis now that he finally showed up for work." I shrugged.

A gusty breeze swished through the tall grass, jostling the narrow-headed cattails that framed the creek up ahead. We steered toward the muddy banks and paused before plowing through the shallow bottoms. The horses splashed, their hooves squelching deep in the mud and grass on the other side. I pulled my reins tight and slowly fell in behind my brother, watching his back.

"It's because he's got a woman. That's the only reason he's been gone so much lately. It has to be." Tripp turned his face up toward the sun and smiled as soon as we crossed the water.

"Not Memphis! I can see drugs or gambling addiction but not a woman. Memphis loves his freedom too much. He'd rather cut out all his tattoos than be tied down to a woman."

In the distance, Abilene's pickup truck barreled down the winding road and over the hilltop before disappearing. I cleared my throat and swallowed hard. The taste of scalded coffee still lingered, fresh in my mouth. When I finally tore my gaze from the road, Tripp stood still on his horse, watching my reaction. The harsh wind, coupled with his fear of water, had whipped a rosy color into his cheeks.

"Speaking of," he started, "Josie said you and Emma Jean are competing against each other in the Blue Ribbon Championship. Something about you wanting to win a massage from her."

"Wait. What? You mean to tell me she's also their resident massage therapist?" My brain whirled inside my head at the possibilities of being naked in a room with Gillibrook's most desired bachelorette. I wiped a dribble of drool from the corner of my mouth and sent a mental note to my johnson to calm down.

"Yeah. That's what Josie said Emma Jean did back in the city. I thought you knew. I thought that's what this whole thing was about. You wanted her to rub and tug you like that damn massage chair back at home—Ruby."

"Buffy."

"Buffy. Anyway, are you really going as far as trying to win this damn competition to corner her into a conversation while you lie on a table, naked?"

"*We*. We're going that far. I need a partner for one of the categories. That's where you come in," I said as casually as possible.

"What?" Tripp's voice rose an octave. "You want me to race? That's this weekend! I haven't prepared. I got to run laps and stuff! Look." He pinched a small belly roll that hung just above his tight blue jeans and shook it at me. "Ever since Josie came to town, my middle's been growing a little bit. She feeds me too many pastries. I can't run a race!"

"Sawyer's competing in the bull-riding stuff, and Memphis won't be around. You're all I got! And besides, we gotta be there all day anyway. It'll be fun. You don't have to run. It's not that kind of race. It's different stuff. We only need to compete as a group in one. The rest I can handle on my own." I clicked my tongue and steered my horse toward our neighbor, Marley's, land. The scent of burning leaves drifted over from his place, filling the air with a hint of autumn bonfires.

"So, I have to look a fool just so you can have a night at Buck Off, bucking off with your high school sweetheart who broke your heart over a decade ago." He galloped beside me, spitting out the words through stiff lips.

"Who said anything about bucking off? Besides, I'm acting as gentlemanly as I can about it. She'll see if she ever gives me a damn chance. But I have a feeling she won't back down. Not Emma Jean," I said before turning toward him. "It means a lot to me to clear the air. Damn memories have been stuck in my head for years. You know what that's like, don't you?"

He let a stifling silence fall between us before answering, "Fine! What races do we have to do then?"

He sighed with exasperation but not before I caught a flicker of mischief in his eyes.

"I'm going to fly solo for a bunch of stuff. But we're going to do something simple, like the Barnyard Olympics probably. I don't know. I need to look it up on the committee's website and see my options. I've not had much time to think about it. I've been busy."

"Busy doing what? The competition is in a few days, and you don't even know what you're doing! How do you expect to win? I bet Emma Jean has it all planned out already. She's going to roast you."

"You think so? Can you ask Josie?"

"Oh, no. Uh-uh!" He wagged his finger through the air. "Don't come to me for cheats through my girlfriend. We don't want a part of this. But I imagine Emma's dragging her into it, just like you're dragging me. You two were made for each other!" He rubbed the back of his neck, pulled out his phone, and began to text. "Hell! You two high school drama queens are roping us into these petty games. I ain't won a thing in my life, and now, I gotta go up against my girlfriend!"

"You don't know that for sure! Maybe Emma's teamed up with someone else."

"Oh yeah?" He shoved his phone out toward me. "I'll be damned."

I grabbed it and brought it to my face, shielding the screen from the sun. A photo of Mama Sue, Abilene, Emma Jean, and what looked like an upright coffin with the words *Gasket Casket* written across the top loaded slowly over our spotty signal. Josie stood to the side, flexing her little lump of a bicep and smiling.

"Fuck! They're doing the outhouse races. We don't have enough people for that. Do we? Think we can do that with just me and you?" My voice broke, edged with a sudden rush of anxiety I hadn't anticipated.

I handed his phone back to him and rode off, quickly inspecting the fence so that I could finish my work, return home, handle my Marie situation, and prepare for my competition.

"Does it matter how many team events you need?" Tripp yelled, catching up to me.

"The brochure said I just needed to win at least one team race and two solos. It didn't say anything specific. But I guess group games are counted same as solo, too, then. Shit!"

"What about Marie?" he asked.

"Really? Do you think she wants to team up with me to win a night with my ex-girlfriend? Besides, I'm breaking that off tonight. Not that there was ever anything to break off. But …"

"Wait. Back up. There's something between you two? I thought you were just friends!" He pulled his reins, slowing his horse from a steady gallop to a cautious crawl, as if he could tiptoe over this conversation entirely.

I slowed, matching his speed to explain.

"There's not! That's what I just said. Or at least, there wasn't yet. I took her on three dates. Really two. The other was just a movie with her daughter. I felt bad for them and all. But nothing ever happened in the bedroom. The closest I ever got was a kiss on the cheek. I did brush up against her breasts once, and I think she thought it was on purpose."

"Was it on purpose?"

"Yes. Until … Emma Jean showed back up in Gillibrook,

and then I slowed down. But, tonight, I need to hit the brakes and come to a complete stop."

"That was your friend's wife! And you're upset over the Kyle and Emma situation ten years ago? Damn. You and Emma have so many partners and drama. I can't keep up."

"I'm trying to fix that."

"How? What're you going to say to her after you finally get her to talk to you?"

"Stay. I'm going to ask her to stay."

"I didn't even know you still had feelings for her. Hell, you've got a woman on every street. Why Emma?" He swatted a fly buzzing near his ear.

"Because she's my Josie. She always has been. What we had back then, I haven't been able to replicate. I've tried. You know that. But those women on every corner have never come close to the fire Emma sparked in me. We were just too young to know how to handle it back then. I like to think we're more mature these days, but she's building a Gasket Casket, and I'm about to steal a turkey for the Fowl Rodeo event."

He put his hand up, stopping me. "Okay, okay. All you had to say was, she's your Josie. I'll help you, brother. When are we kidnapping the turkey?"

"Now. Let's hop the fence to old man Marley's place and see if we can find one in the hills before Dad and Memphis come looking for us." I looked briefly over my shoulder and knocked my boots against my horse, speeding away.

Tripp followed closely behind, gurgling a terrible attempt at a turkey call in the back of his throat. I threw back my head and mimicked him before we both nearly fell over in a burst of laughter. His love-struck mood was catching. I only hoped Emma would stay long enough to catch it too.

I TURNED on the shower and let it run until it grew warm while I laid the raw steaks out on the counter. Tonight, Marie had secured a babysitter, and I had some explaining to do. I just hoped she wasn't too far gone with fantasies of our future that I would send her spiraling into another heart-break. She didn't need any more drama after all she'd been through, and I didn't want to be the one to bring her down again when I finally felt she was emerging from grief. I knew the signs.

I'd grieved the loss of my brother Cole and my grandparents' sudden deaths. I'd grieved for my old dog, who had been my best friend for fifteen years. I'd grieved for my brother Tripp, who fought the battle of depression for almost half his life until Josie rode in on her big yellow bus. And I'd sure as hell grieved my relationship with Emma Jean. I wasn't a stranger to grief. But there was one person I would never grieve for, and that was Marie's scandalous husband, Brett.

I'd met him one night at the local saloon, Bushwacker, when the owner introduced us. Brett was in the market for a pony for his daughter's birthday. He pulled a picture of Marie and Katie up on his phone and showed it to me, beaming a broad smile from ear to ear. We'd ended the night with a couple of beers and a scheduled meeting at my ranch, so I could show him a thing or two about horses before he made the big decision to purchase one. I'd witnessed too many unwanted animals end up in rescue—or worse.

If there was anything I protected in this world more than my family, it was my love for my four-legged friends. Horses and I understood each other more than any human relation-ship I'd ever had. I didn't need to speak to communicate with them. Scooby, my horse, was my closest confidant—and my therapist. We'd hightail it out of the barn and into the pastures, where I'd talk his ears off for hours. I'd been doing it ever since I was fourteen and Dana Lynn kissed me behind the big oak tree in her backyard.

Brett had needed to know how special these animals were before deciding his pony was too much work and sent it to the slaughterhouse. So, I invited him and his family over several times, showing them how to groom a horse and take care of it properly. During their visits, they laughed and smiled, giving off wholesome, *great American family* vibes.

That was why, the last night Brett and I met for drinks at a dance club in Weller, I was shocked to find some young woman who looked barely eighteen, riding the pony—on his lap.

He introduced me to her as if it were nothing. As if we were both womanizers and his little secret wasn't a big deal. Sure, I might have often boasted about my more than fair share of women. But I wasn't a cheating bastard. Still, I brushed off his transgressions until I was clearheaded enough to think our friendship through. But the drama kept coming, turning my stomach with each sick admission. He spilled the beans on the multiple affairs he'd committed over the years, showing me pictures of naked women on his phone for proof. I struggled to keep my cool, but there was one thing my father had taught us Miller boys from the time we could stand. It was the same skill set Abilene had taught Emma Jean. We knew when to hold 'em and when to fold 'em. Our poker face skills were unmatched.

I stayed late that night, listening to Brett's disgusting stories while mentally making a list of every rancher within a five-hundred-mile radius to dissuade his purchase of any animals. He wasn't getting a pony—that was for damn sure. If he treated his family like scum, I could only imagine what he would do to an animal. But the fabled Miller luck was actually in my favor for once, and Brett never returned to Gillibrook. He had drunkenly plowed his car straight off the side of Mount Odina after his confessions. I never shed a tear.

Instead, I'd swooped in like an eagle, protecting Marie and Katie from the truth. The last thing they needed was one of Brett's many girlfriends to show up at his funeral and crush them both. So far, no one had publicly come forward with Brett's *other* lifestyle, and I would never say a word— another skill taught by my good ol' dad. We kept our noses clean and out of everyone's business. Our secrets died with us.

I undressed, tossed my dirty clothes into the hamper, and stepped into the warm shower, letting the scalding water wash away my weariness from the task ahead. But I hadn't even grabbed my cracking bar of old soap and washed my balls before a commotion started up from outside. A burst of shouts barreled back and forth, slicing through my tranquil escape like a machete. I quickly turned the shower off and grabbed a towel, wrapping it around my waist and rushing out my front door, soaking wet.

"You could have killed me! You're so fucking selfish!" Sawyer screamed from the middle of our gravel drive. He'd jumped off of his horse, and he stood beside Memphis's motorcycle, throwing his hands out to his sides.

Memphis revved his engine, popping his muffler into a loud echo. Sawyer's horse whinnied.

In the distance, Tripp ran toward us with our giant turkey tucked under his arm.

"Me? Selfish? The spoiled baby of the family is calling *me* selfish? I told you I couldn't fucking do it today! You knew I couldn't! So, don't start fucking whining because you didn't get your way and I didn't show up!" Memphis planted his boots on the ground and stood up, straddling his motorcycle.

Sawyer grabbed his cowboy hat in his palm and threw it

on the ground. "Baby? Baby of the family? You think I've had it easy?" He let out a snarl.

Memphis swung his leg over his bike and hopped off before sliding his foot under the kickstand. He spread his arms wide, beckoning Sawyer's advances with a mocking grin.

"Hey! Hey! Cut it out!" I rushed toward them, wincing with each stomp on the jagged rocks under my bare feet.

Sawyer cut his eyes to mine, silently pleading his case that I knew nothing about. We all knew Memphis wasn't like the rest of us. He was as stubborn as a mule and didn't fall in line with the family bond drilled into us. If our father told Memphis to turn left, Memphis veered a hard right.

But Sawyer wasn't a walk in the park either. There was truth to Memphis's statement. My youngest brother had always had it easier than the rest of us. Our dad never scolded him or toughened him up as he had with his other sons. Sawyer was the showman of the family. The one who he sent out into the world to represent the Millers. He wasn't a recluse like Tripp, a rebel like Memphis, or a man-whore like me.

"What's going on?" Tripp shouted, nearing our circle.

The turkey squawked a nervous *gobble*, stretching its massive feathers out over Tripp's arms.

We'd caught the varmint quickly because the damn thing was too big to run fast. I had reservations about putting him in the Fowl Rodeo because he was clearly out of shape and would not win us the prize. But Tripp had promised to condition him over the next few days with a strict regime, and not wanting anything to do with our fat, feathered friend, I'd happily obliged.

"What the fuck are you doing with a turkey?" Sawyer groaned, putting his hands on his head before dropping them to his sides.

"That's not important. What's important is, you two are making a scene, and I'm about to have company. So, either take this shit somewhere else or drop it." I secured my towel around me tighter and pointed my finger at Memphis and Sawyer. Droplets of water clung to my brow, dropping into my eyelashes and blurring my vision. I swiped my forearm across my face.

Memphis shot me a look of death, piercing the distance between us with his alarming sky-blue eyes. It didn't matter how many times I'd witnessed that resentful expression cross his face. The look in his eyes made me shudder, not because their color stood out like a turd on snow, but because I knew what lurked beneath them—a torturous existence. As much as he pissed me off, I always felt bad for him too. Blood was blood.

"Oh, I'll fucking take it somewhere else. Come on then. You want to throw down like you're the big shot? Let's go. Your place or mine." Memphis tipped his chin toward Sawyer's place up the road.

Sawyer's chest sporadically moved up and down with deep, racking breaths.

Gobble. Gobble. Gobble.

"Christ!" Sawyer turned, picked up his hat, and dusted the brim. "You're not worth it. This place is a circus. Always has been!"

"Don't say that!" Tripp said, dropping his jaw and cuddling the turkey into his chest.

The fat, feathered beast's talons scurried rapidly beneath his grip. I second-guessed my lack of faith in him.

"Now, we agree on something," Memphis growled, hoisting himself back onto his motorcycle.

"Good." I looked between Sawyer, Memphis, Tripp, and the turkey.

Only the turkey was brave enough to meet my gaze.

Sawyer blew out a breath and climbed back on top of his horse, sticking his middle finger in the air before galloping away. Memphis returned his salute and sped off toward his cabin. Tripp, the turkey, and I stood in their dust, watching until they disappeared.

"Those two will never get along," Tripp muttered.

Josie's bus rumbled down the road, kicking up a plume of dirt behind it. Behind her, Marie swerved her van, narrowly avoiding a prairie dog scurrying down the lane.

"Shit. She's early." I turned on my heels, sprinting back toward my cabin.

"Wait! What about Sawyer and Memphis? Are you going to talk to them? What about Sir Von Himperpoot?" Tripp held the turkey in the air. It spread its wings and stared me down.

"What?" I paused, looking over my shoulder.

"That's his name," he said, shrugging.

"It really is a circus." I ran my palm down my face. "I can't be big brother all the time. Memphis and Sawyer will figure it out. And Sir Von Whatever is in your hands, remember? You said you were going to train him!"

"I was until Waylan thought he was supper! The dog nearly chomped him whole. If it wasn't for Sir Von Himper-poot's perplexing flight skills, this poor bastard wouldn't be here. You have to take him!" Tripp jogged toward me, thrusting the turkey in my arms.

"Are you kidding me? Shit! Marie's just about to be here, and I haven't even finished showering! What the hell am I supposed to do with it?" I wrestled the turkey in my arms. Its talons scratched across my middle, sending me howling.

"Hold him tight! Hold him tight! He just needs to feel secure, and then he'll stop struggling." Tripp brushed a soothing touch over the turkey's head, immediately calming Sir Von Shithead.

"Damn it!" I squeezed the daylights out of the turkey, holding him steady, and ran back inside, setting him on the floor. "Don't move!" I warned him.

I rushed toward my closet and shoved my legs through a pair of jeans before slipping a wrinkled T-shirt over my head. I was still damp from the shower, but I didn't want to give Marie any flirty vibes if she showed up and I was only wearing a towel over my waist.

Ding-dong.

"Coming!" I yelled, running toward the front door.

Sir Von Nincompoop had somehow flown up onto the counter. He stood atop the steaks, pecking them into a meaty, shredded mess.

"Oh my gosh!" I hurried to him, swiping my hand across the counter and shooing him away.

He landed on the floor with a *thud.*

The doorbell rang again.

"Just one second!" I picked up the turkey and shoved him in the pantry, shutting the door behind me. He squawked in protest.

"West?" Marie's voice called from the porch.

I skipped over a pile of turkey droppings, mentally cursing Tripp, and answered the door.

"Hey, Marie! You're early! I haven't yet showered. If you can just—" I started.

"West, I'm leaving. I'm so sorry to do this to you. But Katie and I have to go." She glanced behind her.

I opened the door further and stepped outside. Katie sat in the backseat, surrounded by suitcases and bags stuffed in every inch of the van.

"What? Now? What happened? It's so late," I said.

The turkey gobbled from inside.

"Is that a turkey I hear?" She pressed her fingertips to her collar and scrunched her brows.

"Yes. Long story. But why?" I searched her eyes for any signs that she'd found out about her husband's double life.

"Have you ever felt something nudging you in a direction? Like a strong force telling you to go before something happened? Or something telling you to stay for something amazing?" she asked. Her lids slipped down over her eyes.

"Can't say I have. I've always been content with doing what I do now. Staying here with family. Whatever happens, happens. No one persuades me to pivot. But then again, I'm not still enough to listen." I took a step forward and waved to Katie before returning my gaze to Marie.

The direction of her conversation was as familiar and unnerving as some of the ideas Tripp used to try to explain to me.

"Well, I've been still ever since Brett passed, and I keep hearing a voice, telling me to go. It's this town, I swear. Something about it. It just listens. It knows. It directs." She lifted her voice, barely above a whisper. "I know that sounds crazy. Years ago, I wouldn't have believed it either. But now, it's a feeling, much less a thought. Something is protecting me, I guess. It's telling me to leave. Now."

I swallowed hard, edged with little control. This was possibly the best outcome I could have asked for, and yet I felt like the shittiest excuse for a human being.

"What about Katie and her art contest? She was looking forward to that. You can't stay through the weekend?" I asked. My breath burned raw in my throat.

She blinked rapidly, holding back the tears bordering her eyes. "I can't. This doesn't feel right. You knew Brett, and it's just not going to work. Besides, my mother has been asking me to come home anyway. Now is as good a time as ever, right? I don't have anything here. This town is getting rid of me for some reason." She brushed her fingertips under her eyes and wiped them on her pants.

I nodded. The wind picked up, raising the hair on the back of my neck. Marie's hair blew about her, framing her face into a sullen memory I would have etched in my mind for the rest of my days.

"Understood. Can I at least tell Katie good-bye?" My voice shook.

"Of course! Come on." The tight lines in her face relaxed. She waved me toward the van and turned away.

I followed her down the porch steps to the passenger-side backseat of her van. Katie's lips turned down into a pout as she rolled the window down and shot me a gut-wrenching, teary-eyed gaze.

"We have to leave, Mr. West. Mama says a storm is coming. One we can't see. We can't get caught in it. I don't know what that means, except I can't enter my drawing into the fair." Katie held her drawing in her lap, pinching the corners between her tiny fingers.

"Just because you can't make it there doesn't mean we can't enter it! Give me that." I held out my hand. "I'm entering it for you! And when you win the grand prize, I'll ship it to your doorstep. How about that?"

A twitch of animation wrinkled her nose, curling her lips into a grin.

"Really? You'd do that?" She perked in her seat and handed me the drawing.

Beside me, Marie shifted on her feet. Her eyes clouded with tears.

"Mama?" Katie's smile faded again.

"I'm fine, honey! Promise. It's happy tears." Marie dipped her head and walked to the other side of the car, sliding into the driver's seat.

"I'd love to enter your drawing in the competition. I know you're going to win it. And as soon as you and your mom settle, she'll text me the address, and your prize will be on the way!" I said, pressing the drawing to my chest and patting the car door with my hand, as if I could tell the van to *giddyup* before my eyes clouded.

"Thank you," Katie whispered, glancing at her mom in the rearview mirror.

"It's been my pleasure, Miss Katie. When you get big and famous, don't forget me now. I'll want an original print of yours hanging above my mantel one day."

I stepped back, walking backward, and waved good-bye to Katie before shuffling toward Marie's window.

"You sure this is what you want?" I dropped my voice, leaning into her.

"I don't know. I just know it's what I have to do," she said, biting her lip. Her makeup flowed down her cheeks in watery black streaks, and she wiped away the inky smears.

I shriveled with emotion before remembering my poker face and rigidly holding myself in check. I'd only cried in front of others a handful of times in my life, and this wouldn't be one of them. I'd proven to be strong for them both thus far, and I would send them off with solid confidence, no matter how fake it felt. They deserved better.

"You're a good man, West. I'm glad Brett had someone like you in his life to talk to before the accident. He wasn't very open and communicative. I think that he struggled with that. I know you two hadn't known each other long, but I'm glad he had you to confide in. Or talk to. Or whatnot. I know his travels for work kept him stressed. He didn't like to bring that home to us, so I'm sure he let it all out on you." She tried to smile but failed.

"I'm an ear for you too, you know. No matter what. You call me anytime—day, noon, or night. I'm here." I ran my free palm over the hood of her car. "Did you check the oil before you left?"

"Just like you showed me."

I nodded, taking a deep breath.

"Thank you for everything. I mean it."

She pressed her lips together and held her emotion inside, bottling it up in an all-too-familiar fashion. I'd often done the same.

"Text me when you get home? I'll need that address to send Katie's prize." I held out Katie's drawing and gently shook it in the air with a victorious wave.

They both grinned, teetering on the edge of laughter. But the heavy sorrow filling their abrupt good-bye prevented any of us from emitting even a faint giggle. I knew I'd never see them again. Marie curled her palm on the stick shift and put the van in reverse. I stood back, giving her space.

"Good-bye, Katie!" I lifted my voice above the crunching gravel under their tires. "Good-bye, Marie."

"Bye, Mr. West!" Katie called back, frantically waving her hand out the window.

Marie's resistance vanished as she let out a sob and fled.

I knew grief. Even when it snuck up on me like a storm, washing over me in waves I never expected.

CHAPTER FIVE

EMMA JEAN

I SWISHED MY HAIR BACK IN FORTH IN MY HANDS, WORKING IT up into a messy bun, and dropped down at the kitchen table, nearly collapsing. I'd stayed up late the night before, prepping my massage room and conditioning myself for today's events. This week, I'd prepared for a war I didn't have the energy to fight. But I wasn't a loser. And after my walk of shame back to my hometown, all of Gillibrook would have their eyes on my unfaltering winning streak—or my train wreck of a downfall.

I couldn't give anyone the satisfaction of seeing me fail, and neither could my mother. She'd bristled as soon as I told her West was tracking me down again, and to avoid that drama, I had to enter—and win—the Blue Ribbon Championship. When I'd broken the news of the predicament I'd gotten myself into, she had gone straight to work, coaching me like she had in my yesteryear's beauty pageants. She'd stayed up with me all week, working on different tactics for each competition, whether I wanted to learn them or not.

"Mornin', sunshine," Mama Sue said.

She sat, dressed to the nines in her pressed rodeo shirt and blue jeans, sipping a steaming mug of coffee across from me. Her thin lips twitched with each long sip of spiked brew she took. Her elderly innocence was merely a smoke screen. I could smell the heavy-handed shot of whiskey hiding beyond the brim clear across the table.

"Mornin'." I covered my mouth and yawned.

"Ah boy," she sighed, taking a swig from her drink and blowing out a breath.

She reached for the basket in the center of the table and picked through a pile of muffins until she found one half as big as her head. Her fragile hands trembled as she hoisted it up, inspecting it. She already had a basketful, neatly packaged in clear cellophane and tied in red gingham ribbon, for the fair's baked goods competition.

"Presley special?" I raised my brows at her mug.

"This mornin's no time to be playing around, hon. Your mama's fit to be tied with you and this competition. She's already got my feathers ruffled. So, yep, Presley special this morning. One shot of whiskey down the gullet, and I've got fire in my belly and my soul for the entire day. You should try it. Lord knows, you need it." She pulled down the muffin wrapper and inhaled the crumbly top before taking a bite.

I rubbed my temples with the tips of my fingers and thought for a moment about downing a shot before giving up the notion. As much as I needed a fire under my ass, whiskey on an empty stomach left a sour taste in my mouth.

I chose my words carefully, pressing for an overdue conversation while my mother was out of range. "I don't know why Mama's so anxious over me winning. Ever since I was a babe, she's always pushed me to cut my competition like a hot knife in butter—ruthless and vicious."

Her thin fingers tensed around her sticky breakfast pastry.

"Ah, fiddly piss. That's what it takes to win. You ain't all ruthless and vicious. I've seen you gallivanting with plenty of men. And any guest who walks through the door immediately takes to your charms," she said between mouthfuls while scraping crumbs into a pile.

I folded my arms across my chest and leaned back in my chair, glancing behind me to make sure my mother wasn't listening. But it was Saturday, and I knew by her unfailing routines, she was out for a morning ride.

"All that tough-girl stuff leaked into every other part of my life, ya know. Boyfriends especially. You might see me gallivanting with men, but here I am at thirty, without a durn ring on my finger. I don't want to get too close, or they'll break me," I said.

"Honey, if you're not willing to ride the high of a man who loves you, you're already broken."

"Because she broke me in like a bronco in the hands of a Miller rancher." My voice trailed off as I realized I'd mentioned my competition.

But it was true. If anyone could break an unruly horse, it was the Miller brothers—just another reason I didn't want West to get ahold of me.

"Your mother's still got some healing to do." She put a hand up before I could protest. "Even after all this time. She pushed you to make your way in this world the only way we women around here know how—by toughening up and fighting. However," she said, dusting a crumb from her shirt, "you're thirty without a ring on your finger because that's what you chose. All these men around here, and you find a flaw with every single one of them. You can't blame your mama for that. Maybe you should lower your standards just a bit, honey. They don't make 'em perfect. Life isn't a beauty pageant. Stand up onstage long enough, and you're bound to notice flaws."

"I know no one is perfect. I'm far from it. I'm just scared to get close, is all. Besides, I have met a perfect man— Grandpa. He was tough as nails but still had a tender heart."

"Can't argue that. But men back then were a different breed." She balled the empty muffin wrapper in her fist and set it on the table, flicking a crumb from her lip with her thumb. Her hooded lids slipped down over her eyes, peering over me like she'd study a textbook. "You know, your grandpa and I weren't always perfect either." Her tone grew impatient.

"What do you mean?"

"I resisted him for a long time because, well, I wanted the bad boy. I needed to jump on the back of a motorcycle and make out behind the shed. Your grandpa, he wasn't like that. He drove a sedan and held the door open for me. On our first date, he brought two bouquets of lilies. One for me and one for my mama." Her eyes twinkled, catching the morning sun filtering through the window.

"Wow. That's really sweet. Did you settle with him then? Since you gave up your motorcycle-gang dreams?" A shot of despair rippled through my chest as I prepared myself to unravel more family drama I'd wish I hadn't learned.

"Hell nah. I loved every moment of my time with that man. But I didn't know it until I gave him a chance. I was bent on leather and ink, but my passion really lay with lilies and lace." She reached for the lace trim along her collar before clearing her throat. "I still have a flair for the dark side though. Don't get me wrong. That's why I can't stay out all damn day at this fair. I got to be home to see my vampire soap opera, so I'm driving myself today."

I breathed a sigh of relief. "Okay, okay. Thanks for telling me about grandpa. I really miss him. I hope when I do get that ring on my finger, it's from someone as special as him."

"I do too, dear. I know the way he left us tore us all to pieces. But don't lump his departure from this world with the deadbeats who chose to leave, like your dad. Grandpa would have loved to stay." She shook her head and turned toward the window.

A long, brittle silence filled the room. Outside, the sun blazed orange, casting a warm glow over the pasture. Peckerdoodle strutted across the driveway, crowing for the one guest who was still fast asleep upstairs.

"I know. I wish he were here to help me out today."

"Your dad?" she asked, turning her attention back to me.

"Heck no!" I said. "Grandpa. I know he would have helped me build the Gasket Casket or prep Peckerdoodle for the races. He would've had a grand ol' time. He used to teach me to win too, you know. But have fun too. Mama's different. She tells me to win or else."

"Them two butted heads when your mom was a youngin too. She's never been able to open up much, especially after her divorce. Your mom's stubborn—I'll give her that. But just look at all she built. She's got an empire, and she did that by not putting up with any bullshit. And she didn't do it for her. She did this for you." She gestured with a sweeping motion of her arms.

I glanced at the copper pots hanging from the ironwork above the granite island, the massive stainless steel refrigerator, and the custom built-in oven and stovetop etched with our horseshoe symbol. When I had been a little girl, we'd had none of this.

"But this isn't me. I didn't want this. I wanted a job in the city. A real city. Like New York or something … not Weller."

Tommy's face flared in my memory at the mention of the city.

I'd dated that douche for a little over a year while he traveled back and forth between cities for work. I should have known when he never committed to staying more than a week at my place that he was a flight risk, just like me. I'd played the same card more than once. Except, with Tommy, things were different. When I was away from Gillibrook's prying eyes, I did let myself feel and become vulnerable. And just like what I had thought would happen, I'd ended up brokenhearted over a man who was too cowardly to even tell me good-bye.

"And I wanted a motorcycle man. But guess what. I got something better because I gave it a chance. No one was as shocked as me when that happened. So, give something—or someone—different a chance. Throw this game or let West in. Hell, let your mom in. Don't run from your roots like you run from hard emotions. Your mom might be stubborn, but she never ran. She faced her fears head-on. What she taught you was to protect yourself. I know it wasn't her intention to teach you to run. There's no bravery in that even if you do always win the race somehow."

"What's that supposed to mean?"

"It means that you can't make all men pay for the mistakes of a few. Take that boy West, for instance. Look at what all he's doing to get to you. Lord, have mercy, because he is battling it out at the county fair just to win a chance to talk to you, and you shut him down over what? A mistake you made ten years ago and a fear of letting him inside that head of yours? Sometimes, I think I'm the only broad around here with a lick of sense." She rolled her sleeves up and wiped her hands together. "You and your mom think you're different from each other. But you ain't." She rose from the table, finished her cup of spiked coffee, and held it in the air for an invisible toast. "They don't call it truth syrup for nothing."

"How so?" I eyed her empty mug, suddenly hankering for a shot of firewater myself.

"Your mama was in here, ranting and raving earlier too. Same line of conversation, just in a different direction. But she got her panties in a wad and left." She carried her cup to the sink.

"You mean, she was ranting and raving about me? Figures. I bet she thinks I'll lose and embarrass her or something. Good thing I'll have her there to command me." My mood plummeted at the anxious thought of my mother's drill-sergeant attitude carrying me through the competition.

She turned around and leaned back on the sink, resting her thin-skinned knuckles on either side of her hips. "No, she's not going. And that's why she's nervous. You got it all wrong. She didn't want to leave you today because she thinks if you don't win, you'll run. Your mom wants you to stay home on the ranch. She misses you even if she has a hard-wired dumb-as-shit way of not admitting it."

"Really?" My lips thinned with uncertainty.

"Of course, really. She's your mom. She doesn't show her love through baking cookies and singing hymns. She shows it through teaching you how to navigate the rougher side of life even if she fails at it often herself. She might be a mother, but she's a cutthroat cowgirl at heart too. She was hoping to instill that wisdom in you, but I told her she didn't have to work so hard at it. It was having the opposite effect on you, like you just confirmed to me. You don't need to learn to be tough. You're a Presley. You were born with it."

"Did she have anything to say about that?" I massaged the nape of my neck, releasing a threaded tension building in my muscles.

"No. Course not. So, I started in on how you run because you two are both stubborn mules, and guess what."

"What?" I swallowed hard.

"She told me she came to me for advice, not an ass-kicking. She said our little talk sucked, and then she got on her high horse and ran," she spit the words out, nearly thrusting out her false teeth before popping them back into place and wiping a bit of drool on the back of her jeans.

I covered my mouth with my hand, holding back a burst of laughter. "She did not! Did she really tell you it sucked?"

She wagged her bony finger in the air. "Like mother, like daughter. I should know. She's got my crude mouth."

A stab of guilt buried in my chest for my harsh judgment of a woman who had tried her best in the only way she knew how. She'd never once admitted she missed me or asked me to come home. Abilene Presley didn't show feelings like that, and neither did I. But I'd turned my anxious thoughts into rants this morning, and she'd done the same. That was something at least.

"Well, I'll be darned. At least I didn't inherit that. How distasteful." I stuck my nose in the air and tossed my hair behind my shoulder before rising from my chair. "Now, let's go win this son of a bitch."

"See? It's in your blood, darlin'." She curled her fist into a finger gun and shot it into the air before blowing it out.

I repeated the gesture with a wink.

"For Mama. And me," I responded matter-of-factly.

Mama Sue gave a curt nod and disappeared down the hall.

My mind grew languid with the skills my mother had taught me and the newfound reasoning behind them. Blood was blood. I couldn't let my mother down even if I had to pretend I planned on staying home a little longer before I took off again on my own high horse.

I PARKED beside Josie's bus and stepped out of my mom's old, rusted truck and into the grassy field, already packed tight with vehicles. Dozens of canvas tents lined the horizon, situated in between even more food carts. Smoke curled from their grills, permeating the air with the scent of bacon-wrapped turkey legs, sickeningly sweet cotton candy, and greasy, deep-fried everything. My stomach knotted at the thought of a corn dog slathered in mustard as yellow as the dirt floor after the corn-shucking contest.

I'd only had enough time to scarf down half a muffin while driving before I gathered my lady balls and quieted my nerves. My grandmother's admission of my mother's moment of weakness this morning had caught me off guard, giving me more pressure to win this Blue Ribbon Championship than I'd previously had. Competing against West was exhausting. But competing against my mother's expectations was nearly impossible.

Josie marched over to me with her arms crossed over her chest. Behind her, Tripp scurried on her heels.

"I told you, you have to fall back! Not forward. You can still trust me!" Tripp said.

"Emma Jean, have you ever done a trust exercise?" Josie's nostrils flared as she skidded to a stop in front of me.

"I don't know what you mean." I scanned behind them, spotting the Miller Ranch horse trailer.

West's jet-black cowboy hat bobbed up and down as he led his horses out, handing them off to a young hand waiting nearby the livestock tent.

"You know, like when someone tells you to fall and they'll catch you," Josie said.

"Maybe when I was a kid. Why?" I drew my attention to

Tripp, who stood, running his palms up and down his face, groaning.

"Because, yesterday, we were at the lake, where I used to attend summer camp, and I was telling Josie about the trust exercise they'd made us do. I wanted to show her. So, I told her to fall," Tripp said.

"And I fell straight into the water! He didn't even catch me!" Josie pointed her fingers to her eyes and then to his, narrowing her brow.

"You have to fall backward! Not forward! Who does that?" Tripp threw his hands up in the air.

"I don't trust you today, you little weasel. Emma and Mama Sue and I are going to kick your ass!" Josie stood on her tiptoes and peered over my shoulder. "Where's Mama Sue?"

"She'll be here later with Peckerdoodle. She wanted to drive herself, so she could leave before her vampire soap opera came on at three." I shot Tripp a sympathetic look and returned my gaze to West.

He moved in long strides, effortlessly guiding the horses' reins down the ramp and to the other side of the trailer. I watched as he whispered to them before patting their rumps and sending them away. He reached for his hat and pulled it off while tousling his thick hair back and out of his eyes. I ached to run my hands through his hair like I had at this very same fair twelve years ago. A heat wave surged from my fingertips to my toes before I remembered that West was my competition, and his mesmerizing ways weren't going to be my stumbling block.

"Earth to Emma," Josie said, smiling. "You sure are in la-la land a lot these days!"

Tripp stood beside her with his one lone dimple winking back at me. Both of them swayed in unison.

"Sorry, I was just eyeing up my competition." I flushed,

studying an airplane flying overhead to keep my heart from throttling.

"Sure. Sure. Well, just so you know, West is primed and ready." Tripp wrapped his arm around Josie and pulled her hip to his, whispering something in her ear.

She looked at him and smiled, nodding her noggin like a wonky bobblehead from the ninety-nine-cent store.

"Ah, okay. Good. Me too." I put the matter aside and began working my way across the grassy parking lot. "Josie, you got the Gasket Casket in the bus, right?"

"Aye, aye, captain!" She gave me a quick salute.

In the distance, an air horn sounded, followed by a gruff voice on the loudspeaker. "Event competitors, step right up to the midway tent! Step right up and make sure you get your name down. I repeat, event competitors, make your way to the midway tent. The events begin in one hour."

West scanned the parking lot from across the way until he landed on us, making our way toward him. He pulled his mouth into a sour grin, waving at me with long, dangly fingers.

"Oh, well, will you look who it is? She did decide to show after all. I guess this is one predicament you ain't running from!" West called out as I approached him like the gracious pageant queen I'd once been, although I sure as hell didn't feel like it in this moment.

"You're going down, buddy!" Josie raised her foot in a kung fu kick and flexed.

Tripp beamed, a proud smile stretching across his face. I winced at their matching grins.

"The only thing that's going down is …" West's gaze lazily trailed down my collar and exposed midriff before settling on the tight crotch of my jean shorts. He snapped his eyes back to mine. "Your palms on my slick, oiled-up … *back.*"

I twisted my mouth. At this moment, I wanted nothing

more than us to be going down—at the same time—on the massage table back at the ranch. But West was risky. He was a mixture of passion and heart that, try as I might, I couldn't handle. My rigid walls wouldn't allow it.

I replied as icily as I could under his intense magnetism, "I think you're quick to forget how I play to win."

I took a step into him, bunching my fists at my sides and curling my claws into my palms. I lifted my gaze to his and offered him a cool stare, but the heat growing within my body flickered, igniting more than my competitive streak. My breaths became ragged, uneven, and sputtered out in a hoarse whisper, giving away what little resistance I harbored for him.

His tight expression relaxed into a smile. He reached for my shoulder, running his strong, callous palm up and down my skin and sending a trail of goose bumps down to my trembling legs. Tommy Pickins hadn't had man hands. His dainty hands had been soft, well-manicured, and hadn't worked worth a damn between my thighs. But West had working hands. One flick of his wrist, and I knew those fingers would fly over all of my buttons, rough, raw, and needy—just how I wanted it.

Beside me, Josie began to fan herself frantically.

"Don't worry. I'll console your first loss when I cash in my winning prize at Buck Off. I'm good with heartbreak. I can teach you a thing or three. Besides, I'm really looking forward to Mama Sue's breakfast and finally having that conversation you've been skipping out on for … oh, I don't know … is it eleven? Twelve? Thirteen or so years now?"

"You don't mean what I did with your best friend, Kyle, right?" I pulled out all the stops, switching my emotions off and focusing on winning, no matter the stakes.

Josie and Tripp both sucked in their breath.

Shots fired.

"Event competitors, please line up in the midway tent. The events will begin shortly!" the gruff voice once again called over the loudspeaker.

West stumbled back, thinning his mouth with displeasure. "I'll see you at the finish line." The trace of laughter in his voice vanished. "And then I'll see you at your house. That is … if you're brave enough to stay," he said, a fragile thread of warning deepening his tone. He smiled with smug delight and tipped his hat in my direction.

"Let's go make sure we're signed up. Come on." Tripp pulled West's elbow, leading him away.

"Ooh-wee! Holy jelly doughnuts! You two need to borrow my bus for a bit? I could cut that sexual tension with a karate chop!" Josie said, rocking back on her heels when the Miller brothers left, out of earshot.

"What?" My mind whirled, swirling with doubts.

West wasn't giving up easily. And talking about feelings and what had happened with Kyle was the last thing I wanted to do—ever. And it wasn't because I felt guilty about it all either. It was because, like my grandma had said, I was stubborn. I didn't owe West anything, and the second I felt I owed a man something, I'd quit living free. My mama had said so.

"Emma Jean?" a voice called from behind me, rudely interrupting my thoughts.

I stopped in my tracks, frozen. I knew his voice in an instant. The familiar way my name rolled off his tongue was what had led me into this mess in the first place. It ricocheted off of me like a firecracker—beautiful and dangerous all the same … just like him. The hair on the back of my neck stood on end, as if reaching out to him before I could even turn around.

"Kyle," I answered, turning toward him and breathing out his name like a prayer.

Lord, have mercy.

My heart thumped in my chest at the sight of his chiseled jaw and well-muscled frame. Back in high school, he'd been well on his way to rock-star status with his rippled six-pack abs and masculine butt chin. And today, his extra forty pounds of steely beef along with his rugged beard and inked-up arms confirmed that he'd reached that status long ago. Texas, or wherever the hell he was living these days, had been damn good to him.

I peered over my shoulder, making sure the Miller boys were still walking away before returning my attention to the massive beast standing in front of me. I caught an intoxicating whiff of sweat clinging to his fitted white shirt. The damp material clung to every ripple across his chest, giving me a peek at the tattoos hiding underneath. He smelled like leather, sex, and enticing bad decisions.

"Fuck. I get it now," Josie whispered beside me, just low enough for me to hear. "I bet riding him was like riding a motorcycle—dangerously delicious and leaving your crotch sore after."

"You've no idea," I whispered back, staring at the man slowly disarming my confidence with his filthy grin as memories of our short time together flooded my resolve, fading my competitive streak to a distant thought.

"What're you doing here?" I cleared my throat.

"I'm here, visiting my parents for the weekend. I'm still in Texas. I never left after college. But my parents just bought a place in Jackson Hole and wanted me to check it out. I figured I'd stop by the old stomping grounds while I was here. I never expected you to be here though. You still look every bit of a beauty queen. You competing today?" he asked.

I waved my hand in a fluster. "No. Too old for that now."

"Yes, you are! Yes, she is!" Josie stepped beside me, hooking her arm around mine. Her bony elbow knocked against my hip. "But not in the beauty pageant. She's going for the Blue Ribbon Championship. We've got to compete in outhouse races, and … what else did you sign up for? You're racing Peckerdoodle, right?"

"Well, I'm not signed up for all the races yet," I said through gritted teeth. "That's why I was heading to the midway." I gently tugged her toward the fair, hoping she'd take the hint.

"Oh yeah! Crap, we'd better sign up. Like, now." She yanked my arm like it was a limp noodle in last night's stir-fry.

I rubbed my shoulder and shook her off.

"I'm so sorry to rush away like this. But I have some important events I have to attend. Rain check?" I offered him a noncommittal smile and slowly backed away, as if I were dodging a bomb, which I was.

I knew I was powerless to resist his raw sex appeal. In our brief dating period, we'd barely come up for air.

His skills were exactly how anyone would expect if they judged a book by its cover. And his cover screamed a vicious fantasy that hurt so good. No one had touched me like Kyle had—ever. I'd tried and failed several times at finding someone who could toss me around like a rag doll, but so far, no one had measured up. Not even the rough and tough cowboys who claimed they knew the ropes.

One time, back in the city, I'd joined a motorcycle club just to flirt with the possibility of being railed by an outlaw who would fuck me like he'd just escaped from prison. But even that was a doozy. The only play I'd gotten into there was a stubby, little fingerbang from some wannabe biker named Lloyd. I hadn't even finished before he got a hand cramp.

"We'll catch up! I can cheer you on from the sidelines." He winked, flashing me a grin.

I dipped my head and turned away, following behind Josie.

"Did he just wink? Jeez Louise! He's a motorcycle man who winks? I bet he dirty-talks. He has to. I've read all about this type in my romance novels, and to be clear, those are kind of my favorite—aside from the cowboy smut, ya know. But put me in horny jail because if I were you, I'd let Kyle rummage my sausage wallet anytime." She marched through the parking lot and over the pavement toward the midway tent.

"Did you just say *sausage wallet?*"

"I did." She raised her voice above the shrieking kids on the Tilt-A-Whirl circling the track nearby. "Heard that's what all the kids call it these days."

"Has anyone ever told you that there's never a dull moment with you?" I asked, picking up my pace before she lost me in the crowd.

"Tripp. That's why I love him—and you! So, saddle up, bitchacho! We have a competition to win. Don't let Mayor McNasty back there throw you from the game. Hell, if I stood in his presence any longer, he'd throw me from the game, too, and I got a man."

We made it to the midway tent entrance and ducked inside. Tripp and West were at the front of the line, filling out paperwork. Sawyer stood off to the side, waiting. The brothers exchanged grins, laughing and joking with the other contestants around them. My confidence spiraled at the thought of Kyle's arrival and the small-town drama that was about to unfold.

I looked for the nearest exit and contemplated a run, but

Mama Sue's scolding voice rang loud in my thoughts, reminding me to stay. I was committed and determined to see the trials through, no matter the outcome. Even if the entire town watched as our decadelong war came to its final battle and my reign as the Heartbreak Queen came to a dismal end.

CHAPTER SIX

WEST

I sent Sawyer away to enter Katie's drawing into the art contest while I prepared for the milking competition across the fair. It had been years since I'd milked a cow, but my confidence in my magic hands led me to believe this was the one event I'd easily ace. I could fumble my fingers across a set of teats and make all the ladies squirt. Milking a cow wasn't much different. All I had to do was squeeze and release, and I practiced that move on the daily.

"You sure you know what you're doing?" Tripp asked, pushing through the crowd.

"Yeah. Memaw used to have us do this all the time back on her farm. I reckon it's like riding a bike—you never forget. Are Josie and Emma here?" I craned my neck, searching the crowd.

"Nah. They're prepping the Gasket Casket. The only competitions you both entered are the Fowl Rodeo and Barnyard Olympics. Josie showed me their schedule, and Emma's doing the Talent Competition, Llama Costume,

Baking, and I forget what else. You two won't have to see each other and butt heads all day, I guess. I kind of like the tension this competition has built between Josie and me. This week has been fire in the bed! I never knew she had such a competitive streak. Mmm." He rubbed his jaw and smirked.

"I bet she's riding on Mama Sue's coattails for the bake-off. What a cheat! And I know she'll win the talent show with her voice. She always won the singing competition in her beauty pageants. Fuck! Where did she get a llama though?"

I made my way toward the end of the arena, stopping in front of the biggest heifer I could find. If this cow wasn't a prime milk bank, I didn't know what was.

"No idea. But Josie seems confident they'll win this thing. And you … you ain't looking so hot there, buddy." He scuffed his boot on the dirt floor, glancing left and right. "Marie left you with a void, didn't she?"

"How did you know?" I folded my arms across my chest and stood next to my cow, waving away any other contestants likely to steal my prized specimen.

"It's written plain as day across your face. I saw her pull up at your place the other night, and I watched her go just as quick."

"Yeah, well, she moved back home. She said she needed to get out because she felt a storm coming. Whatever that means." I avoided his gaze.

"She's right. I feel it too. It's like the air is charged with electricity. Something is brewing at the edge of Gillibrook. It's been hanging in the air all week. Even my dog's been hiding under the bed."

I gulped back a ragged breath and shuddered. Tripp was an old soul and wise beyond his years. Whatever had changed inside of him when he lost his twin put him in tune with the universe in a way I couldn't and didn't want to understand. I wondered if it took losing someone you had an intense connection with in a senseless tragedy to put a person in touch with a world that most couldn't see. But any relationship Marie had had with Brett was fake. At least, on his end.

I ran my palm down the cow's spine. Her soft, bristly hair scratched against my skin. She mooed, stomping her hooves impatiently. I shushed her with the same soothing tone I used on my horses, calming her into submission. She settled with a flick of her tail.

"Ahem." I cleared my throat, returning to the conversation. "You ever had to carry a secret around for so long that your shoulders started to feel achy and heavy?"

"Yep. It's exhausting. But that's the Miller way, ain't it?"

"Yep. I just wonder if whatever lurking in the air has anything to do with it. I knew things about Brett that I wish I didn't. Anyway, in a way, I'm glad she's gone. It's good for her. I just didn't expect to be hit with a wave of sadness when she and Katie left. I did care about them." I lowered my voice as the arena grew eerily quiet.

The rest of the contestants were already squatting on their stools, awaiting the signal to start milking.

"Sounds like they moved to better pastures. Just like you're about to do too. You'd better get down there and start tugging those teats," he whispered, tipping his hat toward the cow's underside and reaching in his front pocket. "But take this first. You're gonna need it today. Hell, the whole town might need to carry a talisman for whatever's coming." He handed me a four-leaf clover, laminated into a wallet-sized card.

I smiled before securing it in my shirt pocket with a pat across my heart.

"Take your seats!" a man's voice called from the loud-speaker, echoing throughout the stadium.

Tripp waved good-bye and darted off toward the bleachers, squeezing in beside two teenage girls decorated in rainbow face paint. Behind him, a child let go of a balloon and began to wail as it drifted to the rafters.

"On your mark. Get set. Go!" the voice yelled, followed by an air horn's long toot.

"Shit!" I dropped down on my stool and scooted the metal bucket under my heifer before I noticed my cow's bulging, veined milk bag hung low, tapering into two normal-sized nipples and two nubbins half the size of a gherkin pickle.

The fabled Miller lousy luck had come to haunt me, gnawing through my confidence.

"For gosh's sake!" I cried, pinching the nubbin between my thumb and forefinger and giving it a little shake.

The cow mooed, shifting her weight from hoof to hoof.

"Shh. Hold still!" I kept massaging the stunted teat until finally, a squirt of milk echoed off the bottom of the rusted bucket. "We did it!" I laughed, yanking on a normal udder with my other hand.

All it had taken was a pinch and shake, and my cow's wonky teat shot out as normal as the rest of them.

Until it didn't.

"What's going on? Why'd you dry up?" I bent down, putting my face to the nub and inspecting it.

A fresh layer of milk barely covered the bottom of my pail.

The cow let out a loud groan and spewed a trickle out of her other teats. I grabbed them in my fingers and went to work, rhythmically draining her working udders. Her two nubbins had sucked back up into her and stuck out, only the size of two shriveled popcorn kernels. I paused to wipe a bead of sweat off my brow and returned to the task.

I yanked both working teats until I was red in the face, sweat pouring down my collar like a whore in church. But still, I'd hardly put a dent in filling the pail, and the clock was quickly ticking, setting my nerves on edge. I decided to try to smooth-talk her into cooperating, like I did all of our animals back at the ranch.

"Listen, ma'am. You see, I really need to win this thing. I know you don't understand because you're a cow. But right now, you're the only thing standing between me and a romp in the hay. So, what do you say? Can you just push it out or something? Help a cowboy out here."

The cow snorted, drying up completely.

Shit.

The crowd began to count down from ten. The event was already almost over, and I'd only managed to fill less than a quarter of my bucket.

Three.

Two.

One.

The air horn blasted throughout the arena again.

I grabbed my pail and gave my cow a sorrowful pat on the head. "Thanks for trying, I guess."

The other contestants hoisted milk buckets into their arms and carefully walked to the judges.

"Well?" Tripp ran up to me as I marched toward the judging station, peering inside my pail. The animation faded from his face. "Oh."

"Miller luck," I muttered as I stopped in front of the judges and shrugged, setting my milk on the table.

"Ah, I see. No worries. There's always the next one. Want to head on over there now?" Tripp asked.

"Which one is it?"

"Fowl Rodeo and then Barnyard Olympics. Last up is Yodel Wars," he said.

"Let's do it." I shot a sidelong glance at my nearly empty bucket and turned to leave.

The announcer's voice came across the loudspeaker, declaring the winner. I gave a halfhearted clap and left the building. Outside, the mouthwatering aroma of Dee's Nuts drifted through the air, freezing me in my tracks.

"Is Dee here?" I asked, searching for any sign of her food truck.

I had seen the way Emma reacted when I was with Dee at the farmers market. One flutter of Dee's thick lashes, and Emma Jean's nostrils twitched, scrunched, and flared the same as they had when her old friend Becky used to flirt with me. I could use a distraction like Dee, and I was sure Dee would love to use me in any way she could.

She'd been after me and just about every other man in Gillibrook since she was fresh on the heels of her divorce. Rumor had it, her ex-husband hadn't been interested in sex, so Dee had been jumping in between beds and making up for lost time every chance she got. I hadn't played with that fire —yet. But the thought did cross my mind anytime she passed me by and wiggled those hips.

"Aye. I saw her earlier. She's just down yonder. Want some food before we go? We got about, eh"—he checked his watch—"ten minutes, I'd say. Sawyer got Sir Von Himperpoot out of the trailer. He should be waiting on us at the rodeo."

"Maybe later. It looks like our jive turkey is going up against that damn Peckerdoodle." I turned my attention to our rivals coming toward us.

Emma had a giant rooster tucked under her arm, and Josie was brandishing a blue ribbon in the air like a flag. Mama Sue lagged behind with a smirk.

"We got it! We got it! Look, Tripp! We won. Some old-lady knuckleheads in a Crone Throne almost beat us! But Gasket Casket has these toilet-paper catapults, and we creamed them! Creamed them!" Josie said, spitting out a pair of plastic fangs. "Vampires. Casket. Get it? It was Mama Sue's idea. I guess she's got a thing." She stuffed the fangs into her back pocket.

"Those old broads used to invite me for cards, but they quit years ago. Lord knows why. Bunch of hens in a henhouse anyway. I had to show them I was still around." Mama Sue's lips pulled back, revealing her freshly scrubbed false teeth—no fangs.

The devious twinkle in her eye sent a shudder straight down my spine and out my rear, like a shaking tail feather on my chunky turkey.

"One to … none?" Emma asked. The rooster squirmed underneath her arm.

"Only because my cow wasn't built for milking. Otherwise, we'd be tied right now, darling. But don't you worry your pretty little head. The Fowl Rodeo ribbon will be mine," I assured her.

"Peckerdoodle is one mean son of a biscuit eater. He's going to eat your … chicken? Duck?" She stroked the back of her feathered friend's head until he squawked.

"Turkey. We got a turkey! And I've been training him all week long. Name's Sir Von—" Tripp started.

"Never mind that." I waved him away before he embarrassed us both, and I leaned into Emma, lowering my voice. "I'll see you in the arena. I've always wanted to know how well you could work a big cock."

She stepped into me without missing a beat. "Oh, I can work this cock. You're about to find out that I've got a mind-blowing skill you won't believe."

Her breath puffed warm against my neck, followed by her rooster's beak slicing a peck across my knuckle.

"Hey!" I jerked my hand back and contemplated throwing him into the vat of grease bubbling beside us.

We stood, sandwiched in between a pink taco truck and a

deep-fried butter stand. The women working the taco truck were bent down, sticking their heads out the window and watching our exchange with curious eyes.

"You gonna kiss her or what?" one of them asked. She had long, curly hair and a baby on her hip.

"What? No. It's not—I'm not—her rooster pecked me!" I stepped away from Emma Jean and folded my arms across my chest.

The women laughed, disappearing back into the truck.

"That's why he's called Peckerdoodle! If you don't watch it, he'll peck your doodle right off! Come on then. We got a rodeo to win." Mama Sue reached out, grabbing the old rooster from Emma Jean, and headed toward the Fowl Rodeo tent across the midway.

Josie planted a quick kiss on Tripp's cheek and skipped after them, still holding her ribbon to the sky and waving it with pride. I stared, mesmerized by the sultry sway in Emma Jean's hips as she left my side. The row of carnies working the games turned their heads as she strolled by, calling out for her to come over to their booths.

"Marie who?" Tripp nudged me with his elbow.

"I told ya, she's my Josie. Even with that fat pecker. I'd take them both."

"Peckerdoodle and Emma Jean?"

"Damn right." I tugged my collar and let out a low whistle, tossing my head behind the tents. "Come on. Let's go the back way."

Tripp followed on my heels as we wound our way behind tents, vendor booths, and food trucks. Garbage toppled over inside plastic bins, piles of molded hay were scattered over the mud, and harsh whispers escaped the side of a hippie van decorated with bumper stickers next to us.

The whispers grew louder, turning into shouts.

I paused, thrusting my arm out to prevent Tripp from going any farther.

"Someone's having a bad day." Tripp dropped his voice to a whisper.

I sucked in my breath and tiptoed past the van, motioning for him to follow. Out of the corner of my eye, I could make out two figures standing next to the van. My curiosity got the best of me as I quickly turned my head to catch a glimpse of the devious spectacle.

"Holy shit. That's our brother!" Tripp yanked the back of my arm, causing me to nearly topple backward.

Memphis was leaning against the van, face-to-face with a tall woman dressed in a gauzy, flowing dress and flip-flops. Stacked beaded bangles dangled from her wrists as she shook her hand in his face. They were both breathing heavy, ragged breaths, as if they'd been arguing all morning. But even I could sense the sexual tension between them. Their argument seemed like pent-up lust to me. I knew. I'd been there.

"Memphis? Everyone okay?" I asked in a grudging voice.

Before we'd left for the fair, he'd told us he had plans. From the looks of it, I guessed his plans were standing in front of him, waiting for him to give her an angry kiss.

He pulled back from the lady and stared at me with round eyes matching the late summer sky. For once, they didn't look vacant. But the shock left his face as soon as he noticed who had called his name.

"Problem?" he asked, eyeing Tripp and me. The purple vein in his neck pulsed.

The woman arched her thin brows and looked from me to him and back again, puzzled.

"Can I help you?" She balled her hands into fists and rested them against her hips.

"Nope. I don't reckon you can. Carry on." I hurried past in silence, refusing to speak until we reached the tent.

"Well, I'll be damned. You were right! He does have a woman. A carnie!" I lifted my hat and scratched my head.

"You think? They looked mad at each other to me," Tripp said.

"That was sexual tension. Whatever's going on, it wasn't anger."

"Like what you and Emma Jean got. Pretending you hate each other but you still want to rip each other's clothes off and all. Y'all have a funny way of showing one another you're interested. Speaking of, there she is right there. Already at the starting line and right next to Sawyer."

"Shit!" I picked up my pace and ran to Sawyer.

He held the massive turkey on the ground. It scurried its tiny legs, struggling underneath his grip, etching track marks in the dust.

"You're the only dumb bastard with a turkey. You know that?" Sawyer's boyish grin downturned into a spiteful scowl.

I scanned the other contestants, counting three ducks, eight chickens, a hissing goose, two unidentifiable varmints, one peacock, and that damn Peckerdoodle.

"Don't talk like that about Sir Von Himperpoot. He's going to win this race. Just look at him go! He's already ready." Tripp crouched next to the turkey and took him from Sawyer's hands.

Gobble. Gobble.

"He knows who his daddy is," Tripp said, cooing.

"I thought this was West's race?" Sawyer asked, eyeing me suspiciously.

"It is. It is. Tripp was just helping me train him, is all." I crouched next to the bird, acting as if I knew what I was doing. I didn't.

Tripp had spent the majority of time training the turkey at my place. But the massive beast hadn't taken to me as it had to Tripp. He had been right; Sir Von Pooper knew his owner, and it wasn't me.

Beside me, Emma Jean and Josie put their heads together in conspiring giggles. Mama Sue stood back, chewing on a piece of straw. Peckerdoodle cocked his head to the side and stared at my turkey with beady, evil eyes. I had the sudden urge to make the sign of the cross.

"Ladies and gentlemen! We're about to begin Weller's forty-second annual Fowl Rodeo! I'll introduce the contestants one by one as you take your seats," a man's voice called over the loudspeaker. "First up, we have Lucy Goosey!"

The woman holding the goose held him up for all to see. He hissed, sticking a shaky, thin tongue from his bill. The crowd cheered. I searched the bleachers for any signs of my family, but the only people supporting Sir Von Nincompoop were my brothers beside me. I twisted my mouth and patted the turkey's head as the announcer droned on and on in the background.

"Next up, Peckerdoodle!" he shouted.

Emma Jean scooped the rooster in her arms and displayed it to the crowd like a prized ham. He stretched his wings out far and gave a loud squawk, igniting roaring laughter throughout the stadium.

"Show-off," I muttered, scuffing my boot across the dirt and realizing Emma really did know how to work the crowd and the cock.

"And the only turkey brave enough to show his face this close to Thanksgiving, Sir Von Himperpoot!" the announcer yelled above the crowd's cheers.

"That's you! Hold him up!" Tripp stabbed his elbow into me and shoved the turkey in my hands.

I pulled my attention from our rivals and held him above my head, wrestling to keep him stable. His feathers spread, tickling against my forearms. He shook out his tail, let out a harsh gobble, and plopped out an egg the size of a softball. It crashed to the floor in a splat, narrowly missing my face. The putrid smell hit me like a bag of bricks.

"Oh my gosh," the announcer gasped into the microphone.

The crowd grew silent.

My face grew red.

The turkey grew relieved.

"It's okay! She does that a lot." Sawyer raised his voice, which echoed throughout the room, reassuring everyone that whatever the hell had just happened was normal. "It's the feed she's been eating." He gagged, holding his hand over his mouth, and looked to me for help.

"I thought it was a boy turkey!" Tripp whispered, choking on the smell. "Damn! I have to change her name. Bet she'll have more horsepower now."

"I can't believe this shit." I knelt back down, placing the turkey on the ground and hiding my blushing face.

The rotten egg became nauseating.

Sawyer stooped beside me and shook his head. "What a circus."

I side-eyed my competition beside me, struggling to avoid Emma's reaction. But she had covered her nose and fixed her stare straight ahead. Her eyes were on the prize.

"Right. At the sound of this horn, let the games begin. The first fowl to make it over that finish line wins the race. On your mark. Get set," the announcer spit out the words and tooted his horn before I could gather my thoughts.

"Go! Go! Go! Lady Himperpoot!" Tripp nudged our feathered friend.

She refused to budge.

"Let's go, Peckerdoodle!" Josie shouted beside us.

The rooster stampeded ahead, pecking at everything in its way.

"And here we have Peckerdoodle gaining on Lucy Goosey! Chicken Little and Sir—or I should say, *Ms.* Von Himperpoot are bringing up the rear!" the announcer's voice roared into the microphone.

Spectators rose in their seats, calling out jeers and cheers for whatever bird they'd bet on. The Fowl Rodeo was a hot ticket to empty pockets when a few too many hillbillies had drunk the local moonshine and placed bets bigger than their bank accounts.

"He's not moving!" My voice rose in a panic.

"She! It's a she! And she just takes a bit, is all. She's like a diesel engine. Once she gets going, she'll truck all of these buzzards." He nudged the turkey again, this time sending her flying through the air.

She spread her wings wide and floated in a large arc over the two squabbling birds—Lucy Goosey and Peckerdoodle.

"Oh." The crowd cringed in unison as Lucy Goosey snapped at Peckerdoodle's tail, catching a feather in her beak and pulling it out. She held it in the air, like Josie had held her blue ribbon earlier.

"Oh, Lucy Goosey isn't putting up with any threats!" the announcer said.

Our turkey hopped in giant leaps across the other contestants, stopping only to inspect something on the ground. Two ducks barreled past her, waddling neck and neck.

"Howard and Huey are in it for the win! Look at them go!" The announcer's voice rose through the crowd's deafening shouts.

Peckerdoodle and Lucy Goosey circled each other, throwing out pecks and pokes here and there. The rooster crowed, the goose hissed, and we all screamed.

"Peckerdoodle! Get 'em!" Emma's confident demeanor shifted into frightening territory. She wore a maniacal gaze in her eyes that startled and turned me on all the same.

Mama Sue stirred beside her, pacing with her hands on her hips. Josie sat on the ground, biting her nails.

I hopped on my feet, cupping my hands around my mouth, and shouted like she could follow orders, "Get up, you dumb turkey!"

And to my surprise, she did.

"Himperpoot, jump!" Tripp dug his boots into the dirt and sprang in the air as soon as she turned her attention to us.

And as if on command, she listened. Lady Von Whatever scraped her talons across the ground and worked up a running start before jumping high into the air, majestically floating past the other contestants and landing atop a duck. She rode the poor quacking duck until it toppled over under her weight and fell to its side. But it didn't stop her. She used the duck's flopping body as a springboard, leaping high into the air again and landing with a loud thud on the other side of the finish line.

"We have a winner! Sir—or *Lady* Von Himperpoot! I haven't seen anything jump around like that since old lady Mable caught her man in the cornfields with her sister and chased them both down. God rest their souls. Come get your ribbon, boys," the announcer said before switching off the mic.

"Did that really just happen?" Sawyer asked, rubbing his palm across his jaw and watching the birds still battling it out. A thick lock of hair fell into his eyes.

"Damn it to Bessie! I knew that pompous cock couldn't walk the walk!" Emma Jean marched off to grab her rooster.

Mama Sue and Josie stayed behind, exchanging glances before Tripp sandwiched in between them and began to chat.

I jogged toward my turkey, and my hands clutched around her chubby middle, lugging her to the judges' table. The judge draped a medal around the fowl's neck and handed me a silken blue ribbon. I flashed a grin and stuffed it in my front pocket, right next to the lucky clover. A photographer jumped in front of me, snapping pictures as I posed with my winning turkey and reveled in my triumph against enemy number one.

I scanned the crowd for Emma Jean so that I could gloat. But my excitement was short-lived when I realized my enemy number one was actually my enemy number two. I recognized him in an instant. Kyle, the traitor, stood, barrel-chested and brawny, overlooking the rodeo and focusing on something on the sidelines. I swallowed hard and followed his glare to find Emma Jean and Peckerdoodle huddled in a pout. His eyes flicked to mine, catching my gaze for an instant before he returned his attention back to the beauty queen, slowly making his way down the steps and into our battlefield. Again.

CHAPTER SEVEN

EMMA JEAN

After my rooster had failed to win the Fowl Rodeo, I shifted my sights to the bleachers, but Kyle had already disappeared. I'd felt his sultry eyes on me during the entire rodeo. They'd burned through my drawers, melting the lining in my panties with a not-so-subtle singe. But I couldn't have a distraction from the races. My efforts were solely focused on my cock, not Kyle's or even West's. My mama had a fear of me leaving, but I had a fear of me staying. At least if I won the blue ribbon, it would buy me some time.

"Wait! We still have more events we can win. It's not the end of the world!" Josie pleaded, catching up to me as I grabbed Peckerdoodle and ran out of the tent, dodging any attempts at conversation from familiar faces in the crowd.

Mama Sue hobbled behind Josie, struggling to keep up. I slowed my pace, letting them both fall in sync beside me.

"Darlin', you have plenty more contests to dominate. But I've got to get out of here. My soap's on in just a few hours, and I need to rest. That durn Fowl Rodeo 'bout had me mess my britches. I guess I can't handle that kind of anxiety anymore. Gimme Peckerdoodle. I'll take him home." Mama Sue held her hands out for the rooster.

"Thanks." I gently handed over the bastard rooster that had cost me a ribbon.

"You know, you don't have to run if you lose. You don't have to run if you win. You could just stay and enjoy the fun. You can be stubborn like your mama or admit that there's more at stake here than a prize. It's your ego." Mama Sue lowered her voice and leaned into me, shoving a blue ribbon in my palm. "Let it go. And let that fine hunk of a cowboy in —or I will."

I opened my hand and stared down at the blue ribbon she'd won for the baking contest. My eyes brimmed with tears, but I threw my head back and adjusted my smile.

"Thank you. I'll try," I promised, unsure if I was lying or not. But my pride kept me from arguing that what she had said was gospel. My ego needed a good crack across its backside.

She gave a tight-lipped smile, winked at Josie, and walked away. I stood in silence as my grandma disappeared into the crowd. A burst of wind blew throughout the fair, knocking over empty cups littered atop tables and whipping the tent flaps. Handmade jewelry, clothing, and art pieces toppled off booths as their vendors scrambled to secure their wares.

I glanced up to check the weather, but there wasn't a cloud in the sky. The sun beat down on my shoulders like fire, scorching a sunburn across my freckled shoulders.

"What's next?" I asked Josie.

"Barnyard Olympics. Then, we have the llama thing, and … let me check. I think singing's last."

"Shit. The Olympics? Let's go prep. I need to stretch." I massaged the back of my neck and cut through the game booths, back toward the main arena where we had signed up for events earlier.

"Stretch for what? How hard is it? Are we talking about running and jumping? Climbing walls? Or do I need to army-crawl through a hole and jump over fire? I've always wanted to do that."

"It's basic. Three-legged race, egg-drop thing, and a bunch of easy games like that. They have teams at each station, so it goes by fast," I said, wiping my sweaty palms down my pant legs.

Inside the midway tent, people bustled about in matching team attire. One group wore pink tutus and furry headbands. Another wore lime-green nylon costumes with eyehole cutouts. Josie and I were dressed as plain as day, as per my request. I didn't have time for cutesy games when West Miller stood opposite me on the sidelines with ...

Dee's Nuts?

What the fuck?

"What's West doing with her?" I stopped short of making my way to the starting line.

"I guess she's on his team. Huh. I wonder where Tripp went. Let me go ask." Josie ran off before I could stop her.

I stood on the sidelines, peeking from under my lashes at West's elbow rubbing next to Dee's. She moved slowly, switching her weight from foot to foot. Her body was still tall, trim, and sinewy—with a pencil-thin waist flaring into voluptuous, child-bearing hips. Josie wedged herself in between them and began to question West. He turned toward me, alluding to a massive, self-confident appearance, and pushed his hands deep into his pockets.

I inspected my fingernails and paid him no attention, determined not to reveal my jealousy.

Josie jogged my way and heaved a long breath. "Tripp's

coming. He just had to check on Katie's artwork, so West could prepare."

"Huh? Katie's artwork?" I asked.

"Yeah, you know, Marie's daughter? Well, they left last night."

"Left what?"

"Gillibrook. Marie wanted to go back home, so they packed the van and left. But Katie had her heart set on the art competition. So, West promised to enter it for her."

I blinked, nearly stumbling backward in a heart-rending tenderness that struck me like a chord on Garth Brooks's guitar.

"That was nice of him. I guess Marie and West aren't a thing after all."

"Nope. I guess you're free to … *canoodle*." She wiggled her brows.

I smoothed back my hair and swallowed a lump in my throat.

Across the floor, Dee perched herself up on her toes and wrapped her manicured hands around West's thick forearms before pecking him on the cheek. He watched her leave, bathing her in admiration as she sashayed toward the bleachers and draped herself over them in a pinup pose.

My heart drummed inside my chest.

"I'm free to win this championship, is what I'm free to do. Let's do it." I tore my attention away from them both and scouted out the judges' table, lined with blue ribbons.

Eyes on the prize.

An announcer came over a loudspeaker, calling out team names and sending them to their respective stations. I planted my heels firmly in the ground and stood at attention, waiting my turn. Josie fidgeted beside me, throwing flirty waves here and there to her boyfriend. I jerked my eyes to the other side of the room, where the Miller team stood. Sawyer had joined his brothers.

"I hope we can win this with just us two. It seems everyone else has whole groups," I said.

"If you're talking about Sawyer, he's just watching. Tripp said the organizers split up the groups according to how many are in each team, to be fair." She cracked her knuckles.

"Presley, Abbot, Cox, and Miller, to station four." The announcer commanded my death sentence through the loudspeaker.

"Shit! I bet West slipped the judge a twenty to put us at the same station." My voice drifted into a harsh whisper as I stomped toward station four—the gunnysack race.

"You think so?" Josie asked. A look of enchantment crossed her face as soon as she spotted the oversize burlap sacks piled in a heap.

"I know so." I offered a sneer to West as he stepped up to the starting line.

Tripp made a weird gesture with his hands to Josie and fell in behind him.

"You know the rules, and if you don't, then what are you doing here? This is the potato sack race—or as I and anyone with a lick of country in 'em likes to call it, gunnysack racing. Get in the sack and hobble to the finish line. The first one to complete the race wins a ribbon. Got it? Good," a woman said in a gruff voice, pacing the starting line. She scratched her rear and scanned the other events before continuing, "Looks like we can start. On the count of three."

"Crap." I scurried to an empty sack and dived right in it, pulling it up around my waist like a ballgown. It scratched against my skin, bristling against my freshly shaved legs.

"Looks good on you!" West called from two rows over. He'd inched the sack up to his hips, but the oversize bag barely covered half of him.

"I know," I replied, leaving the competition in the dust as soon as the game coordinator counted to three and blew her whistle.

I'd had a lot of training when it came to getting away, especially with my pants around my ankles.

One time, in the city, I'd been caught stark naked in an alley behind some fancy art gala. Tommy had discreetly rubbed me in all the right ways as we meandered through his friend's modern paintings. But the only thing on our minds that night was newfound lust—the irresistible kind you had when you first started humping someone.

So, naturally, we never made it through the entire gallery. We found an emergency exit, snuck out, and he smashed me up against the wall, pulling my skirt down and taking me from the back. I got in three good moans before the security guard shone his light on us. I never hobbled off so fast in my life. With my skirt twisted around my ankles, I'd hopped down the alley and to the parking lot, naked as a jaybird.

I was pretty sure there was security footage of it somewhere on the internet. But right now, I didn't care. It had been good training.

I leaped through the air with short, rhythmic bursts, flying past my competitors. One poor fellow fell sideways and decided to inchworm-crawl toward the goal. He finally gave up and began to roll. West was gaining on me, coming up to my right and shouting out barbed insults that I couldn't quite hear. Something about a princess turd muffin or a hallelujah butt stuffin'. I couldn't make out what he said over the roaring crowd, so I tuned out his jests and kept hopping.

But the second I reached the halfway mark, something tickled the bony knob on my ankle. I kept going, brushing it off as a piece of loose thread. But the tickle turned into a scurry, and the scurry turned into scratchy paws clawing at my leg. I twisted my body in a way I'd never known possible and let out a shrill.

"Ah!" I yelled until my voice grew horse.

I jumped out of my sack and high-stepped my knees to my tits, flinging the offender off. My hands flew down my legs, brushing off whatever had tried to crawl up my shorts.

Beside me, West paused, contemplating his next move. Even in the chaotic confusion of my predicament, I could sense his gears turning. He knew he had me beat.

"You okay?" a voice called from the sidelines.

I turned to see Kyle's hands cupped around his mouth, shouting over to me. The way he held his arms up showed every inch of his flexing biceps. They looked like two meaty turkey legs I longed to take a bite of.

West let out a loud, audible sigh and hopped across the finish line like his life depended on it.

I jerked my attention back to my sack, lying limp on the ground, and shook it out, releasing a shaggy mouse with what looked like an oddly bad haircut.

"I think so," I shouted back and stuffed myself into the gunnysack.

By the time I crossed the finish line, West had already traded his bag with Tripp. His brother hopped by me with a mischievous grin that spelled trouble. I knew the look. I often wore it myself.

"Oh, jeez Louise! I twisted my ankle!" Tripp said before falling over mid-race.

I stopped next to him and knelt in the dirt. West and Josie rushed over to us.

"Let me help you." I pulled his gunnysack down, revealing two ankles that looked perfectly fine to me.

"Ow! Ooh-ee, ow, ow!" Tripp grabbed his knee and rolled over.

"I thought you said it was your ankle!" I narrowed my eyes.

He swiftly moved his hands down toward his foot.

"What happened? Are you all right, babe?" Josie asked, dropping down beside him. Her golden mist of hair tumbled down into his face, and for a brief moment, I caught him flashing her a smile.

"Yeah, I just don't think I can race anymore." His voice grew strained. "I'm so sorry, West."

"It's okay. I wouldn't let you race like this anyway." West rubbed his palm over his stubbled jaw and winced.

"Who in the Sam Hill gets hurt in a gunnysack? Lawdy, boy. Did you ever play football or a sport in your day? I swear." The game coordinator blew her whistle.

But it was too late. A contestant had already crossed the finish line.

"Come on. I'll help you up." West stooped, scooping his arms under his brother's shoulders and pulling him to his feet.

Tripp leaned on West as he guided him to the bleachers. I grabbed my sack, dragging it back to the starting line, and put it in a pile with the others.

"You can go with him. It's okay. I've signed up for plenty of races. West and I can both sit this one out," I told Josie.

"Or"—she toyed with a lock of hair—"you can team up with West on the next few races. Maybe you'll both get a prize."

I stiffened, drawing myself up to my full height. "Josie Thatcher, you little weasel. You and Tripp are conspiring to be matchmakers, aren't ya? I saw the weird little hand forma- tions y'all were doing behind my back." I put my fingers under my ears and wiggled them, mimicking their actions.

"Whatever are you talking about?" She pressed her hand to her collar and dropped her jaw. Her accent had grown thick, heavy, and Southern. "Now, if you'll just let me go fix my man right up, I'll meet back with you in a jiffy. In the meantime, I'm sure you and West can team up. I've already asked the judges."

"You did what? See! I knew it!"

"I mean, in my head. So, it's okay. Did you know my gypsy soul speaks to me sometimes?" She rushed off, disappearing into the crowd.

I scanned the bleachers for any signs of West, but instead, my eyes fell on Kyle. He was leaning back against the wall closest to Dee, carrying on an animated conversation. She threw her head back and laughed at whatever he'd said and then scooted over and patted the space next to her. He grinned, exposing a row of straight, bright white teeth against his dark beard.

"Well, well, well. I guess your ex-boyfriend came crawling home to roost. It looks like he's already been snatched up too." West appeared beside me, standing so close that I could feel his heat ricochet off my skin.

"I'm not concerned with him, or Dee, or you. I'm concerned with winning, and it looks like those two goofuses over there are conspiring to shove us together for the next round. Whatever the hell that is."

"It's the three-legged race." He turned toward Tripp and Josie, who had their foreheads together, giggling. "And I bet they knew it. Bastards!"

"It's fine. Whatever. Let them be all giggly and shit. It's only this race, and then we split. Deal?" I asked.

He took off his hat and wound a hand in his hair before putting it back on. Beads of sweat clung to his brow, giving a subtle glow to his sun-kissed skin. I reached out to him for a truce handshake but awkwardly let my hand fall to my side while giving up the brief notion of teamwork.

"This one race. But afterward, the prize is mine." He

rested a hand on my shoulder, letting it relax against my tense muscle.

A rush of tingles bubbled inside my stomach.

"You can think that, but this ain't my first rodeo, buddy." I plucked his hand from me and backed away on shaking knees.

"Nah, I know that. Ain't mine either."

"Then, let's go, cowboy. Giddy on up." I tilted my head toward the next station.

"After you," he said, sweeping his arm out in a broad gesture.

I mustered up what little sense I had left in me and swung my hips to and fro toward what felt like my final battle. Standing, bonded to West, was a fantasy and a nightmare all the same. When I finally reached the three-legged-race attendant, I explained our predicament. But she waved my concerns away and began to lace two thick, cloth ribbons around mine and West's legs.

"I got it! I got it!" West stopped her as she hovered her wandering fingers a little too close to his own peckerdoodle.

I stuck my leg out next to his and held my breath while his fingers fumbled over my ankle. His thigh brushed against my hip, sending a trail of goose bumps down my legs. I couldn't disguise my body's reaction. He tied one swatch of cloth around our ankles and slowly moved up, linking the other mid-thigh. I eased my knees apart, giving him better access. He sucked in a throaty breath and finished, springing back up beside me with a flash of desire nestled behind a devious grin.

"Did you ever think we would use restraints like this?" he asked, towering over me.

"No," I said, only managing to release my ragged breath once the attendant blew the whistle.

I put my arms out in front of me like a zombie, careful

not to let my fingers touch his. My insatiable lust for him grew into something terrifying, confusing, and downright panic-inducing. Try as I might, I couldn't escape. I was stuck to West Miller, the one man who had always stuck by me, no matter how many times I'd pushed him away, like a fucking rat on a glue trap.

"What're you doing? You're going to make us lose our balance!" he shouted, swatting my hands down.

"No, I'm not! This is making us move forward faster." I jerked my hands back upright, away from his body, as we tried to find our rhythm.

"You're supposed to put your arm around the other. Look, like this." He stretched his arm around my back, locking it against my spine and pulling my waist to his so close that I could feel the rapid movement of his breathing.

My flesh prickled.

"Okay, okay. Let's go! We're already losing," I insisted, scooping my hand around his lower back. I gave his abs a commanding caress with my fingers, bit back my unruly desire, and propelled us forward.

A delicious shudder coursed through his body.

"That's it. Now, we're doing it," he said, matching my rhythm. "Looks like we're about to kick those old geezers' asses. Want to take 'em?" He lowered his voice as we neared two of the older ladies who had shunned Mama Sue in the outhouse races.

"Git 'em." I held on to him tight as he hurtled us forward in swift, giant steps.

He deliberately stretched my hip flexors wide with each move to the finish line, spreading my legs as far as they'd go while passing the competition. A rush of blood hummed through my veins.

But the tattered restraints were barely hanging on during this discreet, dirty little rendezvous game. Before we finished the lap back to the starting line, both pieces of cloth came unraveled and fell to the ground. We'd been so in tune with working up sexual tension together that we hadn't noticed until our legs knocked together and back apart.

"Oh no!" I looked down at the fabric lying in the dirt.

Behind us, two women were stumbling over each other and gaining ground.

He snapped his eyes to mine, impatiently blurting out the words, "Trust me?"

"I-I guess," I stammered with unease.

In the background, Tripp and Josie cheered us on.

"It's 'bout time," he said, stooping low and wrapping his arms around my knees. In one swift movement, he picked me up and threw me over his shoulder, making a run for the finish line.

"West! You know we can't win like this!" My voice jostled with each crush of his boot against the dirt floor as I hung, limp as a dishrag, at his mercy.

"Nah, maybe not. But worth it." His head pushed tight against my hip, burrowing in my butt cheek like a squirrel looking for a nut.

"Hey! Are you motorboating my ass?" I pounded my fists against his upper thighs while staring directly at his own derriere. I wanted to touch it, grab it, shove it down with my palms as he buried himself into me. My lustful appetite grew damn near violent.

"No! My nose itched, and the only thing I could do was nuzzle it with you. We can stop running, and I'll let you go if you want, so I can scratch it, but then we'll lose." His breaths became heavy as we neared the finish line.

"*Ándale!*" I shouted, smacking his rear and giving myself just a slight hint of satisfaction.

I felt his smile against my hip.

We reached the finish line before everyone else, amid protests by all the other contestants.

"Not fair! They cheated!" an elderly man said.

"Our ties fell off! Couldn't help it." West offered a forgiving smile and shrugged.

"Sorry, Miller. Disqualified." The attendant swiped her hands out in front of her and declared us out of the event.

I looked at West and roared with laughter. Tears streamed down my cheeks. "I don't even care. I haven't had that much fun in a while."

"See? Told ya it was worth it." He clutched my hand with both of his and pulled me toward the next station.

His eyes held enough magnetism that if I didn't have my emotionless skill set, I'd follow him anywhere. But instead, I stayed true to my roots. I dug my heels in the ground and resisted, pulling my hand free.

"What's wrong?" he asked.

"Nothing. I just need to go. Look, it's been fun. But I don't think I can do any more today. I'm … forfeiting. I know when to hold 'em, and I know when to fold 'em. Now"—I looked behind me at Josie and Tripp coming toward us—"I need to fold 'em."

"Why do you do that? You're always running away. True to your Heartbreak Queen nickname. Love 'em and leave 'em. Then disappear. Poof!" He spread his fingers wide in a bursting motion. "You don't have to do this, you know. Here, take my ribbons. Win the championship. I know how much it means to you." He pulled two blue ribbons from his back pocket. "Please. Just don't go. Stay. I'm sorry if I tried to push you into talking about the past. It's done and over. All I wanted … all I really wanted was just to have a second shot with you before you left again. The conversation I used to get there was an excuse. Emma …"

He studied my face for a sign of objection. I gave him my familiar look of dismissal.

"What're you running from, Emma Jean?" he asked.

"I don't know," I lied. "But now, I need to go." I turned on my heels and left in a hurry, pausing by Josie. "No time to talk. Not feeling well, but you can still compete without me! Thank you for all you've done." I gave her a quick hug and continued out of the tent.

I didn't stop running until I made it back to my mom's old pickup truck, where I rested my forehead against the steering wheel and let myself cry. I knew exactly what I'd run from—feelings, risk, danger, ego, love. But most of all, West Miller, the only man who could convince me to stay.

CHAPTER EIGHT

WEST

THE SUN HAD SET LONG BEFORE WE PACKED UP AND LEFT. After Sawyer smoked the other contestants in the bull-riding tournament, we began to gather our horses and sneak away during the fireworks to avoid a mad rush out of the parking lot. I left a loser, only one ribbon shy of beating Mable Crenshaw, one of the rusty old bitties who had snuffed Mama Sue back in her card-playing days. But it didn't matter anymore. The fear I'd seen in Emma Jean's eyes was enough to tell me I needed to buck off and mind my own business. I'd at least spoken my truth and told her I wanted another chance, leaving the matter in her hands.

"Is that Abilene's truck?" Tripp asked, slowing our truck on a deserted road near Gillibrook.

Behind us, the horse trailer squealed from brake pads that needed replacing. Just a few times down Mount Odina, and the pads had already rubbed themselves thin.

I craned my neck out the passenger window as our head-lights flooded over Emma Jean, bent over the side of the truck's open hood and using her cell phone as a flashlight. A crescent moon hung low in the sky but couldn't provide much light in these shadowy pastures.

"Stop the truck," I told Tripp.

"Course." He passed by her, pulling our truck and trailer to the side. Our tires crunched through the gravel.

I jumped out of the door and tossed a few beer cans back into the truck that had littered the ground beneath me before weaving through the tall grass toward Emma.

"Hey! You stuck?" I called out before I reached her.

"Nah. I just like stopping in the middle of nowhere and rooting around in this here engine stuff." She glanced over her shoulder and pursed her lips. "You here to cash in on that grand prize?"

"Nah. I didn't win. Sorry to disappoint you. I just like stopping in the middle of nowhere to pick up stranded chicks. You know I got the whole white-knight syndrome going for me. I need to save the princess or something like that." I pulled out my phone and shone its light on her engine.

"That's called codependency."

"And this is called ... we're going to be here all night." I peered at the archaic motor and rubbed the back of my neck, wincing. It prickled, heated with a fresh sunburn.

"I can call a tow truck. That's what I was about to do anyway."

"No, no. Don't do that. Hang on a minute," I told her before running off.

I maneuvered around her truck and jogged back to Tripp, motioning for him to roll his window down.

"What is it?" he asked.

The scent of pine air freshener drifted from the open window, masking the smell of hot pavement. The gillyflowers had long since dried up, leaving us in a valley that smelled like a barn, complete with cow manure and dried grass.

"It's going to be a while. Leave me a horse, and I'll get back home," I said.

"Are you sure?"

"The ranch ain't but a few miles up the street. I can handle it. Go, get Sawyer home. He's tired, and the horses are too." I nodded toward the backseat, where Sawyer rested his head against the window, snoozing loudly.

"Okay." He opened his door and walked to the back of the trailer, unhitching the latch.

"What're you doing?" Emma Jean asked, coming toward us.

"I'm going to attempt to fix your truck. And if I can't, well, my best bud, Scooby, here is going to take us home the old-fashioned way." I led my horse out of the trailer and buckled a saddle around his waist while Tripp hooked its bridle.

"It'd be easier if I just called a tow truck. You don't have to do this." She backed up, allowing Scooby some room.

He looked at her and whinnied.

"Do you know how long it's going to take a tow truck to get here? You'll be sitting here, waiting, either way. Besides—"

A wolf howled in the distance, interrupting my train of thought.

"Okay, okay. Let's fix it and get out of here. I'll follow you home though if we can get it running. You don't need poor Scooby out here with wolves. I got a shotgun under the seat. Mama makes me carry it." She stepped to my horse and ran her palm down his neck, speaking to him in a soothing tone.

I'd rarely seen her with a horse or any animals. Despite living on a ranch, she never seemed the type to work a field or a barn. But watching her with Scooby and the way he responded, I could see she was a natural countrified bumpkin, whether she liked it or not.

"Call me if you need anything," Tripp said, holding his pinkie and thumb out in the shape of a banana and putting it to his ear like a phone.

"I will. Thanks." I waved him good-bye.

He flashed me a grin and two thumbs-up before scurrying away.

"What was all that about? He still thinks he's playing matchmaker, I take it?" She raised her brows in amusement.

"Aye, I think so." I led Scooby to her truck and tied him to the door, so I could get to work. I plunged myself into the hood and began to check the truck's vitals.

"What can I do?" Emma asked.

"Sit there and look pretty."

"Really? You know I'm capable of more than that," she said, blowing out a breath.

"Oh, don't I know it. But really, there ain't enough room under this hood for the both of us. You can talk to Scooby and keep him company. I didn't get my morning chat with him today. He's probably lonely." My voice echoed off the rusty tin.

"Morning chat?"

"Yeah. We talk in the morning. I tell him about what's going on in my life. It's usually a whole lot of nothing. But I don't like to bottle shit up, and I don't have anyone besides my brothers to tell all my secrets, so that poor horse right there bears my burdens."

"What kind of secrets?" she asked.

"Ah, ones I take to the grave."

She scuffed her shoes in the gravel beside us and tipped her face to the moon as it disappeared behind a cloud. Another wolf howled nearby. Scooby perked his ears and neighed. Emma shuffled toward him and shushed him, stroking his back with calm hands.

"We're going to get you home and out of here soon, Scooby. I'm so sorry you have to put up with that knuckle-head and his secrets, acting as a therapist to his womanizing drama."

I jerked my head up, knocking it against the underside of the hood.

"That ain't true!" I rubbed my noggin and cringed.

"Oh yeah? Dee? Marie? And I've heard all the rumors. Bet there ain't a woman in Gillibrook you haven't seduced. And you want to call me a heartbreaker. Pfft!"

"Crap! That reminds me. I have to mail Katie my blue ribbons." I tiptoed over her accusations and re-steered the conversation in my favor—expertly.

"Mail them?"

"She and Marie left."

"Oh yeah. Josie mentioned something like that."

"Yeah. Anyway, I entered Katie's drawing into the art competition for her. She didn't win it, but she doesn't need to know that. So, I'm going to mail her one of my blue ribbons."

"That's … awful sweet of you. I'm a little touched." She bit her lip, nuzzling closer to Scooby. "I can send her mine too. Maybe we can say she won in several categories. Drawing, age, et cetera. She can open it up and find a bunch of ribbons instead of just one. I think that would be a nice surprise."

"Miss Tough Babe has a soft bone in her body. Is that your heart bone?"

"Made from the many hearts I crushed in my earlier years."

"I don't disbelieve it for a second," I said.

My phone buzzed in my back pocket, and I pulled it out.

"Shit!"

"What?" she asked.

"Storm or flood warning. I gotta text Tripp and warn him. Looks like a big one. I bet this is the one he sensed." I paced in front of her broken-down truck, turning my face to the cloudy sky.

"Warn him about what? I don't understand."

"You know, ever since the accident, he doesn't do well with storms and rain and all that. I get notifications on my phone when we're about to get hit with bad weather, so I text him and let him know."

"You still take care of your brother like that?" she asked, still stroking Scooby.

Lucky son of a bitch.

"Always." I forwarded the warning to Tripp. "Family's family."

"Yeah, well, my family isn't like that." Her tone grew empty, devoid of any hope or emotion.

"Mama Sue seemed to be supportive today." I put my phone into the front pocket of my best rodeo shirt that I'd worn for today's festivities, now blotched with grease stains from Abilene's old clunker.

"Let me rephrase that. My *mom* isn't like that." She hid her face behind Scooby.

"Abilene is a tough cookie. But I'm willing to bet, it wasn't always that way. Shit shapes people. Then, people shape people."

Thunder rolled in the distance, sending a chill up my spine.

"We need to get going. Lock this up." I slammed the hood shut and patted the truck. "We're going to be caught in the storm if we don't leave now."

Emma nodded, grabbed her purse from the seat, and paused.

"Think we need a shotgun?" she asked. "What if someone

breaks in and steals it? We don't need a rascally thief with a firearm around Gillibrook."

"Everyone and their mama already has a shotgun around here. Just make sure it's under the seat and you lock up. We have to go. Like now."

Lightning forked over the mountains behind us. She locked the truck doors and hurried to me as quick as a mouse.

"Just what kind of storm is this? We usually don't have them kick up so fast this late in the year." She placed her foot in Scooby's stirrup and hoisted herself over with my help.

"I dunno, but I don't like it. Tripp mentioned feeling something coming. Marie said it too. I'm not in tune with the weather, universe, or whatever like that. If you'd asked me, I would have said it was just a freak storm. But I trust my brother, and he was spooked." I maneuvered myself in front of Emma Jean, nearly kicking her off the horse.

I hadn't wanted to appear un-gentleman-like when she hightailed it on Scooby first, but I was steering this beast. The last time I'd seen Emma on a horse was back in high school when her mama used to make her run the fence, and riding a horse wasn't like riding a bike. You had to get to know the horse and let it read your intentions. I wasn't sure what intentions Emma Jean had, but I had a feeling they were to get away from me as quickly as possible.

"Hold on tight, okay?" I told her as I tightened my hat atop my head.

She wrapped her arms around my middle and squeezed. I sucked in my gut and tightened my abs, aware that I shouldn't have eaten that third corn dog. The heat from her inner thighs pushed against my lower back as she spread her legs wide and scooted in close to me.

"Ready!" She rested her chin on my back, bracing herself.

"Giddyup, Scooby!" I clicked my heels against my horse, and we took off.

He raced down the road, expertly navigating through the dark.

We'd often gone on midnight rides in my younger years when I needed to get away from my domineering dad. Plenty of times, we'd escaped the ranch to camp in the mountains with nothing but a small travel bag and a two-person tent. Scooby loved it just as much as I did because he always took his time on the walk back to the barn instead of hoofing it around, as per usual. One time, he'd even nipped me when I packed our things to go back home.

A gust of wind picked up, whipping against my cheeks. Emma buried her face into my shoulders. We rode in silence, galloping only minutes ahead of the storm. I pulled the reins, steering Scooby left and through the rusted wrought iron gate that led to Buck Off just as the rain began to pelt down on us. Icy-cold droplets struck against my hands, freezing my knuckles raw.

"Shit!" I flinched. "I'm going to head straight to your barn, okay? I can't leave him out in this," I yelled above the deafening sheets of rain.

She threaded her hands together, clinging to me and barely moving.

"Of course," she sputtered out the words into my back, shielding her face from the downpour.

"Come on, boy. Almost there!" I shouted to Scooby as he flew down Abilene's driveway and toward the barn in the distance.

Not a single light was on inside the inn. A bright flash of lightning crackled overhead, snaking out in forks and illuminating the barn. Scooby neighed, skidding to a halt at the door. I jumped off of him and opened the door, swinging it back.

Emma Jean grabbed the reins and let out a, "Hiya," quickly guiding Scooby inside.

I shut the door behind them.

"I can't see shit," she said, stumbling off Scooby's back.

Abilene's horse whinnied in greeting.

"Me neither. I think the power's out. It didn't look like your house had any lights on." I pulled my phone from my pocket and shone the flashlight around the barn, finding an empty stall for Scooby.

She used her cell phone's flashlight, too, helping me get him situated.

"Thank you, Scooby, for getting us here safe." She patted his flank.

He shuffled his hooves in response.

"What about me?" I asked, adjusting my eyes to the dark. "I rescued you, even after you invited Kyle to throw off my game. You knew that would kill any chance I had at winning." I lifted my flashlight in her face, like I was interrogating her.

"Hey! That's not true." She batted it away. "I had no idea he was coming. Besides, he looked preoccupied with your fuck buddy, Dee." She shone her light in my face.

"She's not my fuck buddy," I muttered, squinting and shielding my eyes from her phone. My heart hammered inside my chest, hurtling itself against my rib cage like it aimed to break through and present itself to her as a sacrifice.

"Oh yeah? She looked like she'd ridden you hard and worn you out. The way you looked at her was like … it was like …" She struggled to find the words.

I let her stammer out her words before her accusations became entirely unbearable and I could no longer ignore my desperate attempt to resist such a lucky situation.

I stepped into her, recklessly moving my free hand to her

neck, and pulled her mouth to mine, smothering her last words against my lips. She crushed her breasts against my chest, dropping her phone and clutching fistfuls of my shirt. She explored my mouth with her tongue, warming me from the inside out. I savored the taste of cold rain on our lips. I pulled back just as viciously as I'd started and wiped my forearm across my wet jaw.

"The way I looked at her was nothing like the way I look at you," I said in a firm and final tone, forcing her to accept the seriousness of my situation.

"Follow me. You can get cleaned up in one of the guest rooms. Then, meet me in the massage parlor downstairs at the end of the hall. I heard you liked your massager, Buffy. But I think I can make you feel better than she can," she said in between raspy, rugged breaths. She fumbled for my hand in the dark, curling her icy, trembling fingers around mine. "Looks like you got your overnight at Buck Off after all, cowboy."

Outside, a clap of thunder rumbled, shaking the barn's wooden walls and matching the aching tremor building inside of me, roaring to get out.

AFTER THE FAIR, I smelled like sweat, horse, and this morning's failure. One whiff of my downstairs remix, and Emma Jean would use it as an excuse to giddy on up back out of town. Cowboying was hard work. Cowboying while trying to win over Gillibrook's most eligible bachelorette was a damn near impossible task.

But luckily, I'd done something right. I didn't know if it was the fact that I'd lost the competition, her jealousy of Dee, or if my white-knight complex had turned her on when I saved her from a night stuck on an old country road. I didn't question the turn of events myself. If I opened my mouth, with my track record, I was more than likely to stick my boot in it. So, I left the talking to her and just grunted here and there as Emma Jean showed me to my quarters.

She told me she was going to clean up and tell her mom I was in the guest room for the night. She promised to light a candle to guide my way while I quietly poked around downstairs until I found her massage parlor. I didn't know what to expect, but if all those porn clips I'd watched came true, I was on my way to rub-and-tugville with the most beautiful lady in all of Gillibrook.

Once she guided me through the door and into an empty guest room, she hurried away, and I went to work. I locked the bathroom door, hopped in the shower, and began to sing like a bird. I hummed a boot-scooting tune and swiped a soapy washcloth over myself, lathering my taint and balls for a good two minutes before rinsing the suds down the drain. I'd never showered so fast in my life. I had been waiting years for this moment, and the anticipation of what was to come barreled through me in an impatient rush. I hurriedly dried off and tiptoed downstairs in nothing but a damp towel wrapped around my waist.

I slowly shuffled my feet, reaching out in front of me and feeling my way down a hall. At the end, a barely visible light escaped from behind a cracked door.

"I'll be damned. This is really happening," I whispered.

"What's happening?" Mama Sue's voice stopped me in my tracks.

I clutched my johnson with my hand, suddenly terrified for my wee willy wonky. She stood to my right, a shadowy, hunched figure in the kitchen. Lightning flashed, reflecting off the hanging copper pots above her.

"He won. I told him, let's get this massage over with."

Emma Jean stepped out of the doorway down the hall, motioning for me to come.

"Mmhmm," Mama Sue said before disappearing.

I sensed a smile in her voice.

"Come on, you. What's taking so long?" Emma's voice trailed off in a harsh whisper.

I hesitated before scrambling toward her and jumping inside the lit room. She shut the door behind us—and locked it. The storm raged on in the background, muffling our voices. I scanned the room for any signs of a prank but saw nothing, except a taxidermic deer head on the wood-paneled wall.

"His name's O'Dell." She tipped her hat to the deer head, letting her long blonde locks fall over her shoulders. "Mama couldn't save him from a bear. She had to do it to put him out of pain. Didn't want guests to see him first thing, so she put him in here with me since no one really uses this room."

"I see." I dropped my gaze to her.

She wore nothing but a thin cotton robe and a pair of inviting eyes. Her dewy skin glowed russet under the candle-light, flickering off of a few drops of moisture still clinging to her collar. The thick outline of my cock strained against my scratchy terry-cloth towel.

She took a step forward, letting her eyes linger beneath my waist before speaking again. "There's something you need to know about this table. My ex had it made. It's not a normal massage table. I've yet to test it out though. You're my first."

She stepped into me, bumping into my erection and hooking her finger between my hip bone and towel, loosening the cloth. It fell to the floor. My dick sprang up at attention, ready to go. It had been ready for over ten years now.

"Fuck," she muttered, sucking in a deep breath.

I'd had that reaction before. I tried not to let my girthy third leg go to my head, but it did. Often. Hell, half the time I landed a woman from Weller or Gillibrook, it was because of the rumors. Women talked. I'd learned that early on. Once, a former girlfriend's friend had seduced me into bed with the both of them. It didn't matter if they finally ditched me and ran off together. They'd both still cooed over my fat peckerdoodle.

"Everything all right?" I asked, scratching my head.

"Yep. Just hop up here on the table and lie facedown. Put your dick in the hole."

"Your hole?" I gasped, unused to such crude commands this early on in the sexcapade.

"No! This hole, goofus!" She pulled back a sheet from the table, exposing a round hole near the center. "It's a milking table. Ever seen one of these?"

"I don't reckon I have." I gulped, swallowing a hundred different scenarios and trying to work out mechanics before I hopped on board.

Thankfully, she hadn't asked me to lie on my back. That would have earned her a hard nope before I peaced out of Buck Off for good—maybe.

"I'm not going to hurt you. Isn't this what you wanted?" She ran her palm up my back and down again, caressing it in one long stroke before giving me a playful spank on my ass.

But the reality of the situation turned my brain to mush, and I instantly reverted to caveman mode, only able to offer her a grunt.

I climbed on top of the table and made myself comfortable, guiding my cock and balls through the makeshift glory hole. When I was finally situated, I turned over my shoulder to ask her if this was how she wanted me, but she'd already dipped under the table, and she began to tease me quicker than I could get any words out.

"Oh, damn." I let out a long breath and closed my eyes, resting my head on a pillow at the end of the table.

A charge of excitement jolted through me, spreading my toes wide, as if I'd stuck my finger in an electric socket. And that was exactly what she felt like—a zap to the brain, the dick, the heart.

Her fingers trailed up my shaft, slipping over the thin skin on my sack and searing a path back down again to the tip of my cock. She curled her palm around the base and tugged downward, followed by her other palm and back again, with the same milking rhythm I'd given that poor cow's nubbin earlier.

I raised my hips, fucking the table as she picked up her pace. But the second I felt her tongue circle the head, I was hurtled beyond the point of return. I jammed myself deeper through the table and into the warm wetness of her mouth. She felt like liquid velvet, slurping my dick until I leaked.

"Mmm," she moaned, pausing to dribble and spit on my dick.

Her hand cupped my balls, gently massaging them, while her other hand worked my shaft in rhythm with her mouth. She gagged, only coming up every few moments to catch her breath. My thoughts spun out of control as I imagined her swallowing me so deep that her eyes teared up when my thick cock blocked her airway.

But she wanted it. I could feel it. She devoured me like I'd devoured those corn dogs earlier—ravenous as a starved pig at the post-Thanksgiving slop bucket. Each time she gagged, she followed it with a moan, as if she thoroughly enjoyed choking me down. And then I remembered the way she'd thrust herself into me when I had my hand wrapped around her neck, kissing her back in the barn. Emma Jean liked it rough.

Blood rushed through my veins, flooding me with a

violent need to be inside of her before she roused me to the peak of desire and I emptied in her mouth, filling her up more than that stupid cow had filled my bucket earlier.

"Get over here." I raised myself, letting my hard-on slip out of her mouth.

"What? Why?" she asked from under me.

"Because," I growled, curling my fists, "I want to look into your eyes when I feed you."

She scrambled out from under the table and wiped her thumb across my pre-cum glistening on her lips. Her eyes were wet, smeared with makeup, and pleading.

I gripped her shoulders and pushed her to her knees before hooking my fingers under her chin and tilting her head up. "Look at me when you suck my cock. I want to see your mouth stretched while you struggle to keep me down." I traced my fingertips across her lips, parting them for my entry.

I buried my hands in her thick hair and held her head steady as I eased myself down her throat little by little, testing her skills. She expertly kept her eyes locked on mine, slipping her lids down to half-mast as she opened her mouth and took me in. She was right. This wasn't her first rodeo.

"Ah, yes. Just like that. Just like that." I ran my hand down the back of her head, gently reassuring her while fucking her face.

I watched her watching me until the tension to release became unbearable. I stepped back and scooped my hands under her arms, springing her to her feet. In one quick movement, I untied her robe and let it fall to the floor, next to my towel. She stood before me, naked, wearing only a wicked grin that provoked an insatiable, animalistic desire from deep within my caveman mentality.

I let out another growl and grabbed her ass, hoisting her atop the table and pushing her back. She leaned back on her elbows as I grasped and eased her knees apart. I rested my hand on one side of her, leaning my body over her while I teased her with my free hand's fingers, running them up along her slit. I slid two inside of her pussy and curled them upward, searching for her G-spot.

She arched her back, thrusting her swollen nipples in the air and throwing her head behind her. I jerked my palm up in quick, rough movements, burying my fingers inside of her until her pussy became soaked, squelching a mouthwatering sound each time I finger-fucked her. I pulled my hand back and traced my lips with her wetness before sucking her sweet juice off my finger. She tasted like I'd imagined—indescribable and addictive.

I knelt in front of her and fused my lips to her clit, circling my tongue across it in feathery strokes while gently sucking. She bucked on the table, reaching for my hair and threading her fingers through it. I lapped her up until her legs began to shake.

"I'm not done with you yet."

I jolted upright before she could release her waves inside my mouth and yanked her off the table, flipping her around and bending her over the side. She clutched the table with a death grip.

"Condom, to your right," she said between ragged breaths.

I flicked my eyes to the table on the right and noticed the package of foil for the first time. I tore it open with my teeth and recklessly rolled it on.

"You ready?" I asked, knocking her legs apart with my knee.

"Been for a while." She spread her legs even further, raising her round ass in the air and welcoming me into her soft, voluptuous body.

For a brief moment, my breath hitched in my throat.

She'd confirmed the same feelings I had. We'd both wanted this for longer than we cared to admit. We had stupidly played hard to get for damn near a decade. And now that all that anticipation had come to a head, right here on her massage table of all places, I didn't want this to end. I didn't want her to regret tonight and run. But I couldn't control myself either. I'd waited too long and come too far not to accept her invitation.

I hastily reached for her hands and pinned her wrists together, holding them down across her lower back while I guided my dick inside of her, stretching her out. She gasped, stiffening her body until I buried myself up to my balls. She wiggled, straining against my hands, but I only tightened my grip. I leaned over her, caressing my free hand underneath her taut stomach, over her fleshy breasts, and up toward her neck, where I curled my fingers around her throat and gently squeezed.

I gathered her body to mine, scraping my chest against her silky back while holding her snugly against me. She took the pillow between her teeth and bit down, quieting her moans. I jammed into her repeatedly, driving down harder and deeper with each wince she offered. I slowed to make sure she was okay, but she turned her head and whispered for me to keep going. And I wasn't the type to second-guess a lady's commands. I knew when they said to keep going that it meant to keep going. Switching shit up got her nowhere. I'd learned that from the internet.

So, I let her wrists go and slid my hand underneath her, circling her clit.

She gripped the side of the table and began to move her hips, matching my rhythm. "Don't stop. Don't stop."

I grunted, quickening my pace and flying my fingers across her button as if it were the nuclear code and I was about to be bombed—love bombed. Scorching waves of pleasure began to build from inside me again until I couldn't hold back any longer. Any hope I had to hold back and wait on her to finish vanished into thin air the second she cried out for release. She shuddered beneath me while wave after wave overtook her. I collapsed on top of her, holding us both steady as I spilled out inside of her.

My brain buzzed, my heart thrummed, and if my dick had a mouth, it would be singing "Hallelujah."

Emma Jean wasn't just icing on the cake. She was the entire damn party.

CHAPTER NINE

EMMA JEAN

A NERVE-RATTLING CLAP OF THUNDER RANG OUT, WAKING ME from a dead sleep. I rolled over in my bed, knocking into West and startling myself out of a post-horny haze. He stirred but remained blissfully unaware of my panic attack.

Oh my word.

What in the Sam Hill tarnation did I do?

I blew West Miller and let him ramrod me into tomorrow.

Shit.

After we'd had sex for the third time last night, I'd begun to feel more exposed than ever. He shattered the rigid walls I'd built around my heart with each tender touch and each shallow thrust. He whispered my name over and over, nuzzling into my neckline and breathing out the filthiest appreciation I'd ever heard. His tone hadn't just been suggestive, but also downright dirty, growly, and achingly deep with desire.

I'd tried to avoid meaningful sex and thus avoid any sort

of eye contact or gentle touches. But West wouldn't have it any other way. He wanted all of the above, and he wanted it now. All he had to do was trail his knuckles down my cheek and ask for more, and I happily swung my leg around his middle and gave him the trusty ol' reverse cowgirl. We'd giddyupped until I was sore in the saddle and his massive ding-dong flopped over on his thigh in pitiful defeat.

I pulled the covers taut under my chin and planned my escape. My thoughts whirled in my brain, in tune with the gusts of wind roaring outside. The storm slowly wound down.

"You awake?" West rolled over and propped himself on his elbow, stroking the hair back from my face and brushing his lips across my brow. He caressed the length of my back, prickling my skin with his callous hand.

"Yeah," I answered.

"You scared?"

I weighed the question, tiptoeing around an awkward conversation.

"Of?" I asked.

"Oh."

"Oh? I don't understand."

"Well, I meant, the storm. But I think if you have to ask of what, you might be scared of something else." He settled back into his feather pillow and scrubbed his hand over his eyes.

"What's that?"

"This." He motioned his arms out to his sides, pointing to us both. "Me. You."

I detected a note of annoyance in his tone.

I knew when to hold 'em and when to fold 'em. But putting my cards on the table was a practice I refused to participate in—until now.

"Yes," I said, desperately wishing the pouring rain would drown out the blood humming through my veins.

He rolled back over and draped his arm over me, curling his fingers through my hair. "You have absolutely nothing to worry about. It's me who keeps chasing you down. I'm not running from you, but you … you always run from me. Or anyone. I don't want you to do it anymore. I want you to stay. Give me a chance, Emma Jean. Look, I don't even want to talk about what happened when we were teenagers. I know it wasn't fair of me to be that upset over it after all these years."

I sat up in bed, interrupting him before he could continue. "I didn't mean for things to happen that way with Kyle. He'd mentioned you were dating, so I figured it was okay to move on. Hell, I was seventeen. I didn't know what I was doing. I'd waited years for you to be single, so I could have a shot. Then, when it happened, we both weren't ready," I said slowly, carefully navigating through an unfamiliar, muddy haze of feelings and desire.

He pushed himself up, sitting flush against the headboard. His thigh brushed against mine underneath the covers. I side-eyed his taut abs and rippled chest, briefly reliving the way his muscles had flexed as he hovered over me.

"I wasn't innocent either, I know. I was just so jealous of Kyle back then. He didn't care if you were spreading your wings or leaving town. All he cared about was getting what he wanted. But I cared about you. I wanted more than just a romp in the hay with you. And you couldn't give me that. I understand. I don't blame you for wanting more. But here we are, in our thirties, and I don't have more. Do you? After all your running, did you find it?"

"I thought I had. Once."

"And?"

"And the same thing I'd feared happened. I hadn't wanted my heart broken, and I had fallen right into it. That's Karma for you. Tommy was just the universe catching up to me. All those men I'd written off so easily." My voice trailed off into a whisper. "I came home to roost."

"You're wrong. That wasn't Karma. God, or the universe, or whatever ain't gonna punish you for running away before you become too attached to a man. It knows you do what you do out of fear that you were taught. Hell, even I picked up on it as a teenager. I know you haven't had much of a positive male influence in your life, but—"

"You trying to say I have daddy issues?" I ground the words out through my teeth.

"No. Now, listen. I'm saying, whatever the hell happened with this dipshit Tommy wasn't your fault. It wasn't because you let yourself love. And it certainly wasn't Karma. Have you ever thought that maybe you can have love? Maybe you can be happy? And hell, maybe that's even here in Gillibrook."

I jerked my eyes to him in silent warning that this conversation was growing uneasy.

"Just a suggestion!" He put his hands up in defense.

"I like you much better when your words are muffled between my thighs." I folded my arms across my chest and blew out a breath.

"If you ever want someone who knows you more than you might know yourself, I'm here. You can talk to me. No more Kyle bullshit. We're grown-ass adults. If you want to call me to eat cereal at two a.m. because you're lonely or if you just need a booty call, you got my number."

Another crack of thunder echoed off my bare walls.

"Speaking of," he continued, reaching for his phone on the nightstand, "I need to check on my brother and see if he texted me anything else. He'd texted earlier that he and Josie were at his place and he was fine. But this storm is something else. There's bound to be some flooding. I know he's up, waiting it out."

I turned my head toward the window and watched the edges of the sunrise lighten around the dark clouds. I wondered if he ever grew exhausted from carrying everyone's burdens. The thought of constantly being a caretaker to others' feelings was suffocating enough. I couldn't even take care of my own.

"That's really nice of you to take care of people like that. Marie. Katie. Your brother. You ever get tired of being so strong? What happens when you can't keep it up? Who's going to be strong for you?"

"It's part of the older-brother code. Besides, like I told you earlier, family's family. They'll have my back when I need it too. Tripp would help me in an instant. Sawyer would whine about it, and Memphis would protest just for show. My dad and mom are a given." He tapped his phone. "Shit! Battery's dead."

"Here. You can text him from mine if you want." I grabbed my phone from beside me and handed it to him. "It's got a little battery left. Maybe this damn power will come back on soon."

"Thanks." He took the phone from my hand and turned it on.

A picture of Tommy and me popped up on the screen.

Earlier, I'd received the notification that I had a new memory to review right as the Miller trailer pulled up to my broken-down truck. I thought nothing of it and put my phone away, unchecked. But West's fat thumb had swiped a little too much toward the top and brought down my notifications, opening my photos and memories that I'd rather forget.

He dropped the phone on the bed and pushed his heels into the mattress, propelling himself further upright.

"It's fine. There aren't any nudes in there. It's just stupid Tommy. I haven't yet gotten to deleting his photos." I picked my phone up, swiped Tommy away, and handed it back to West.

"Tommy? As in your boyfriend in Cali?" The blood had drained from his face, casting a ghastly glow in the dimly lit room as he held my phone limp in his hand.

"Um, yes. Why? What's wrong?" I inched closer to the edge of the bed.

He stared at my phone before looking back up at me and clearing his throat. "Nothing. Just wondering your type. What did he do for a living?"

"Traveled, is all I know. I barely saw him in the year we were together. He mostly kept a private life because of his job, which was private too. Some type of government work, so he was always called away and only worked in Cali every so often. He commuted somewhere out of Jersey."

"I see. Long-distance relationship. Is that why you broke up?"

"He ghosted me. One minute, we'd been fine, and the next, he disappeared. It was after a somewhat-serious conversation anyway, so I'm sure he got spooked and vanished."

"Oh."

"So, yeah, about that Karma."

"I didn't say there was no such thing as Karma. I'm sure *Tommy* has gotten his. But you don't deserve Karma. You just deserve someone to give you a reason to look at love a little differently." He carefully placed my phone on the bed and slid off the side, planting his heels on the floor before the sun fully rose.

"Where are you going?" I asked. "You aren't texting Tripp?"

"Seems like the storm is calming, and I can see outside now. I'm going to go over there instead. I've got work to do anyhow. You know how work starts at dawn in places like this," he said, rolling his eyes to the ceiling and avoiding my gaze.

"Oh." I shifted my knees up, hugging them to my chest, and watched as he struggled to pull his pant legs on. They were still wet from last night. "You sure you don't want to stay until there's more daylight?"

His face clouded with uneasiness. "It's been a pleasure, Emma Jean. But I gotta get to Tripp. No telling what kind of frenzy he's in right now. That storm was a doozy I hadn't seen coming," he said while snapping the buttons on his shirt. "I won't stay in your hair anymore though. I'm sorry for all that riffraff I put you through." He situated his cowboy hat on his head, tipping it toward me.

A curt, "Mmhmm," was all I could muster. My volatile reaction was already written on my face. I could already feel a new wrinkle forming between my brows—West Jr.

"I'll be seeing you around," he squeaked out the words as if he was in pain and backed away slowly, reaching behind him for the doorknob.

I folded my hands in my lap, like I'd put down all my cards. This was a game I'd forever sit out.

"See ya," I said, pressing my lips into a thin line as he disappeared out of my room and out of my life, loving me and leaving me.

Karma.

I brushed my palms together and suppressed a sigh for the spark of hope he'd fooled me into believing only a few short hours ago when I was lost in a web of desire.

"Ah, well, she's up!" I told the Devil, stomping my heels on the floor and rising from the bed.

I wrapped the sheet around me and shuffled to the window. The rain had slowed to a mist, hanging like a gray cloud over the valley. Peckerdoodle crowed in the distance, followed by a string of shouts and curses. The rooster was chasing West clear across the yard and inside the barn.

I smirked.

I stayed at the window, awaiting the next spectacle, but when West emerged a few minutes later, Peckerdoodle had already left. He looked left and right, scanning the yard, and breathed a visible breath of relief. He patted Scooby's flank and settled in the saddle, chattering away to his horse. He wore a pained expression, etched across his face, mirroring mine.

Overhead, the ceiling fan began to whirl as the electricity flickered back on, and any hope of West convincing me to stay flickered right out.

"You could have stayed too," I whispered as I watched him gallop down the muddy path and out of sight, taking my splintered heart with him.

My mama was right, and I ... I was just heartbroken.

"Mornin'," Mama Sue said, raising her voice above the ancient coffeepot percolating on the stove. She stood, hunched over, peering inside the oven.

"Mornin'. Are those your famous biscuits I smell?" I asked.

"Sure are. We got one guest checking out today and three checking in. So, biscuits in the mornin', and if you stick around today, I'll have fresh-baked cookies for everyone this evening. Other than that, everyone's on their own. My bunions still ache from yesterday's shenanigans." She pulled off her oven mitts and tossed them on the counter.

"I'm sore too. I guess it was all that racing and pushing the Gasket Casket down the street." I rubbed my lower back and poured a cup of coffee into my favorite mug. It had belonged to my grandfather and still had the chip in it from when a moose had startled him early one morning and he cracked his tooth on the rim. He'd drunk his coffee inside ever since.

"Yeah, that's why you're sore," she said, shaking her head.

I dipped my nose in the steaming mug and hid a grin.

"Good morning." Abilene entered through the nearby side door and leaned against the wall, pulling off her muddy rain boots. "Damn monsoon last night 'bout drowned the entire chicken coop I just had built! It's nothing but a big ol' mud pit out there. Thank heavens the power is back on. Otherwise, I'd have to welcome these new guests with a rude awakening. They're West Coast, so they won't be into roughing it. Probably checking in to drown their sorrows. One of them's men left her at the altar. Another is a mom just looking to find herself again. Shoot, this place will give them the peace they need. But not if we get another storm like that in here! I'll be cleaning up branches and wreckage all morning." She shot her eyes to mine. "And you're going to help me. After we get my truck back."

I stiffened my back against the counter and took another sip of my coffee, holding the ceramic cup with both hands. "How're we going to haul it? We don't have a hitch."

"Where'd that Miller boy go? I was going to ask him to get one from his ranch. I know they have 'em over there." Abilene brushed off her pant legs and walked to the coffee, pouring herself a cup.

Mama Sue busied herself with the biscuits and pretended not to perk up over the direction of our conversation. I stooped down and opened the cabinet beside me, pulling out a bottle of whiskey and untwisting its metal cap, as my mother pushed past me and pulled her phone from her back pocket, placing it on the table. She settled into her chair at the head of the breakfast table and waited for me to answer.

"West left already." I poured a shot in my coffee and took a sip, avoiding her gaze. The whiskey and black coffee hit the back of my throat with an acidic heat before warming my belly.

"Where's my shotgun?" She leaned forward and narrowed her eyes.

"Mama! You can't kill him!" I set my mug down on the counter with a shaky hand, spilling a tiny bit of my drink between my thumb and forefinger. I brought my hand to my mouth and sucked off the sticky residue. My hand still smelled like him.

"Lord, have mercy. Where in the world would you get that idea, Emma Jean? I'm asking because I don't want some rascal breaking into the truck and stealing my weapon," she said, raising her hands in the air in a show of innocence.

Her feigned shock slipped briefly before she adjusted the set of her stern brow and continued, "Cat got your tongue? Why did he run off like that?"

I grabbed my mug from the counter, took a long sip, and let out a sigh.

"Because he's a man," I said, dropping down in the chair next to her.

Mama Sue sucked in an audible breath before hastily putting her oven mitts back on and pulling the biscuits from the oven. The kitchen filled with the scent of bread, butter, and the bitter staleness of a conversation that should have happened ages ago.

"I'm going to let these cool. Be back in a jiffy." She fanned the golden-domed baked goods and hurried out of the kitchen, hobbling on her achy bunions.

Mom pushed herself up from the table and grabbed the bottle of whiskey, bringing it to the table.

"Start talking." She sat down and poured a heavy dose of the firewater in her coffee. "The guests will be up any minute now, and I want to know what my daughter's next move is. You going to have your suitcase packed by noon, aren't you?"

"No," I lied.

I'd packed it before coming down to breakfast. I had stuffed everything I owned, which wasn't much, into my old college suitcase. But no matter how much I tried to busy myself this morning, images of West and what we had done kept intruding into my fragmented thoughts.

"Emma Jean, I taught you that poker face you're wearing right now. You can't fool me."

"I never planned on staying this long, ya know."

"I know. I can see the struggle in your eyes. You want to run, but you have nowhere to go."

I let her words whip me across the jaw before answering, "How did you stay? How did you stay in this house when Dad did that to you? Didn't you want to pick up and start fresh somewhere else? And leave all this pain behind?"

"I tried ignoring my pain once. It only built up and closed me down … for years. Course, I used it for good. It motivated me to get this place up and running as a big ol' middle finger to your son-of-a-biscuit-eating dad. But after a while, it'll wear on you in ways you won't know until it's too late. I think your grandpa saw that on me, and it hurt him. I often wonder if I had something to do with that heart attack of his. No one likes seeing their kids suffer, and he sensed my turmoil without me mentioning a word."

"Mama, you didn't cause Grandpa's heart attack! How can you think that?" I swallowed hard, carefully navigating the trepid waters of our extremely rare heart-to-heart conversation.

Mama hadn't spoken about her dad since before the

funeral. Everyone knew their strained relationship was off-limits.

"Maybe not. But it's part of the reason I toughened you up even more so. I don't want to see you hurt. Your pain is my pain. And I've had enough pain in this life to bear for the both of us. I don't want my daughter going down the same path. I'm sorry if it shut you down or shut you out too. That apology has been a long time coming." She reached for her phone on the table and began to scroll.

"You don't have to apologize for not wanting me to hurt. I get it."

She held the phone up and pressed a button. My grandpa's voice rang out, sending a deep ache inside my chest. My knees trembled underneath the table.

"Abilene, I just wanted to tell you, I love you. Sam's daughter had an accident last night, and it reminded me to tell my loved ones how grateful I am for them. I know we butt heads like two elk during rutting season, but I'm so damn proud of the woman you've become. You might have a tougher-than-shit attitude, but you were born as radiant as the late summer sunshine. I know the world's been cruel, but I see that same sunshine in Emma Jean. Don't let your clouds hang over her head too. You gotta let her make her own mistakes. That's how they learn. I don't talk like this to you often enough, and I'm sorry for it. I guess it's that toxic masculinity or whatever hullabaloo kids call it these days. We all have our shells to break. I'll see you this evening before dark, and maybe we can go fishing, like old times. I miss it and you. Oh, and tell your mama to make some of that banana pudding, will ya?"

My mom turned her face up to the rafters in the ceiling, blinking back tears she'd never let me see.

"When was that?" My voice grew quiet.

"The day he died."

"Shit." I rose from the table and brought the kettle over to her, refilling our mugs. "And you kept it all this time?"

"I listen to it every morning."

"Why now? Why're you all of a sudden coming around to me when, all my life, you've shaped me into keeping people at arm's length, and playing my cards right, and keeping my walls sturdy? Besides you not wanting to see me hurt. Why are you just now sharing grandpa's message with me and telling me you're sorry? I could have used this talk ages ago, you know." I threw back my drink and wiped the back of my hand across my mouth.

"Because, Emma Jean, people don't heal at the same rates. I'm sorry it took me so damn long. I did what I thought best at the time. Now, I'm switching gears again. Parenting isn't one size fits all. We grow, same as our kids. You'll always grow. All that rough-and-tough love got you where you wanted then, didn't it? You got your therapist license and even got to try out a handful of passions and hobbies and traveled all over before you ended up back here. You never let one man get in your way of what you wanted."

"I never let one in at all!"

"Tommy?"

"Just him. Only him. A risk I stupidly took."

"West?"

"I didn't let him in. Just"—my cheeks flushed—"further than I thought."

"And he just upped and left like that, huh?"

"He had to check on Tripp. He still gets nervous when it storms, and West still takes care of him. But, yeah, just like that. He ran out of here like a bat out of hell."

"So, you're going to leave now because he hurt your feelings?" She cupped her hands around her mug and twisted it in her palms, circling it back and forth. "I sure as hell didn't teach you to run like this. I taught you how to keep your walls up, but I guess I didn't teach you how to react when some man crumbled them all down."

"I just go away and avoid it all," I said with a shrug. "Onto the next one. It's easier that way."

"How about we do this one differently? Why don't you let me teach you what I know?"

"It's taken you over twenty years to get over Dad. What in the world are you going to teach me about avoiding suffering?"

I felt a stab of guilt as soon as the words rushed out of my mouth, and my mom hid her face in her hands.

"Leading by example. Don't be like me." She lifted her head and looked at me through tired gray eyes, fringed with the long, thick lashes she'd passed down to me. "It's so damn lonely. I tried to teach you to avoid pain while overlooking the pain I was creating. You don't want to be an old maid, mad at the world. Hell, you're right. It took me over twenty years to get over that bastard. I missed my youthful years because I wallowed as a victim, using my suffering as a drive and an excuse."

"Does this have anything to do with you and Brother Roger?" I trailed my finger over the rim of my cup and peered down my nose at her.

"Maybe." Her dewy skin flushed bright at the mere mention of his name.

"Thought so. Of course, it took an act of God to get you to talk like this." I rested my back against the chair and folded my arms over my chest.

Her brows pulled together in an expression of dismay. I'd never seen my mom actively show emotion, and to be honest, the look on her face scared the shit out of me enough to stay the entire year if she asked me to. Whatever Brother Roger had served her had flicked a switch in her coldhearted brain because getting Abilene Presley to bare her soul was a *praise the Lawd* moment. And getting her to apologize was just downright miraculous.

"Like your grandfather said, we all have shells. I'm trying to fix this." She motioned to both of us. "Do you think you can meet me halfway? Maybe stay just a little longer than you planned and spend some time with me? I'll bake cookies, or sing hymns, or whatever it is moms are supposed to do."

"Heavens to Bessie, you ain't burning down my kitchen." Mama Sue rounded the corner, wiping the corners of her eyes with her apron. "I'll do the baking."

"Mom! How long have you been standing there?" Abilene pursed her lips, as if she were about to spit venom.

"You know damn good and well that I was there the whole time! I wouldn't have missed this for the world. Now, let me hear my husband's voice again, and we'll get on with the day. The last thing we need is the guests coming down those stairs to see a bunch of knuckleheads crying into their spiked coffee. You twats need to put on your big-girl panties. Company's coming." She adjusted her false teeth and jerked her head up toward the stairs, where the sound of footsteps grew louder.

My mother quickly handed her phone to my grandmother and showed her how to work Grandpa's message. Mama Sue held it up to her ear and left the room.

"Since I played on your field with your rules all these years, how about, if I stay, we play on mine?" I offered, feeling the stoic effects of whiskey on an empty stomach.

"What exactly are you proposing? You want me to go to a big city and do what? File papers? Ride a subway? Is this a challenge?" She laid her palms flat on the table, stretching her fingers wide before drumming them with an impatient rhythm.

"Sort of. You always called the shots. This time, I'm calling the shots—at the saloon. We go to Bushwacker on

Friday night, and you can even bring Brother Roger if you want as long as you have a good time. That's what I want to see—my mama having a good time. I can't remember the last time I saw you smile. Convince me you even know how to do that, and I guess I'll stick around to see if it rubs off on me." I childishly crossed my fingers underneath the table in hopes that she would say yes.

Friday night was karaoke night, and I hoped to drag Josie onstage with me. Now, if Mama came, I'd have a second backup singer and a fresh start in this rinky-dink town.

"Deal."

"That was almost too easy."

"I have a lot of time to make up for. Besides, I could use a cold beer, loud music, and to shed this weight I've been carrying on my shoulders. Do you think Brother Roger will show up at a bar though? Isn't that against some type of vow?" she asked.

"By the way he looks at you, I think Brother Roger will show up anywhere you ask him."

"Really? How does he look at me?" Her grin stretched into a wide smile, similar to the one I caught on Josie every time she talked about Tripp.

"He looks at you like you're a glass of holy water and his soul's been parched for ages."

A satisfied light sparkled in her eyes, giving her a youthful glow. I wondered what my mom must have been like before the divorce, and I hoped I would get to meet that woman soon.

"So, the same way West looks at you. Maybe you ought to go and—" she started.

I put a hand up, stopping her.

"I chase no man. Any man who's worth chasing won't have me chasing him. He'll show up of his own accord," I said.

She twisted her mouth to the side and nodded, reaching across the table for a high five. "That's my girl."

I slapped my palm against hers and fought the urge to run. For once, I wanted to stay even if it was only to see how this whole church man fit in with my mom's prickly behavior.

CHAPTER TEN

WEST

I SQUEAKED OPEN THE TALL DOUBLE DOORS TO OUR abandoned barn on the south end of the ranch, letting in the morning sun. It washed over the dirt floor and up to the rafters, where droplets of morning dew sparkled along sinewy, stretched spiderwebs. A disturbed flock of birds rustled in their nests before flying out in a burst of annoyed chirps.

"Boys, gather round. This here is going to be our next project." My dad's voice was still gruff with sleep.

Waylan, Tripp's dog, bolted inside the barn, sniffing every corner.

Sawyer, Memphis, Tripp, and I sank our boots into the mildewed straw and stood, circling my dad. Whatever work he had planned, he stalled in telling us.

When he'd banged on each of our cabins before dawn, all he'd told us was to get saddled up and meet at the old barn. Thankfully, I'd already been awake, and I hadn't had to drag myself to the stables.

The last few nights following my departure from Emma Jean's mind-blowing milking table, I'd lain awake in bed nearly all damn night. I couldn't shake the agony of realizing that Emma Jean's ex-boyfriend, Tommy, was Brett. Or that she had unknowingly dated a married man, who was now a dead man. My conscience fought with itself every waking hour on whether or not I should tell her the truth. But then again, I couldn't tell Marie the truth either. I had protected both of them. Marie, by blowing her off until she ultimately left, and Emma, by avoiding her at all costs.

I knew my move was exactly what she'd feared would happen if she let a man into her life. I'd tried to send her a text to ask about her truck, so she knew that she wasn't the reason I'd become distant. I'd played it cool and kept things as friendly as I could until I could sort my options and come to a conclusion over what the hell I was going to do about our awful situation. My thoughts on the entire bullshit scenario, created by that monster Brett, were jagged, painful, and left me with a sick feeling weighing in the pit of my stomach.

I'd wanted nothing more than to have that fantastic night with Emma Jean. I'd dreamed of touching her like that since we were teenagers. But in our several years of torturous, prolonged anticipation, we had gone at each other like wild animals, barely stopping to catch our breath.

I wanted more. I longed to undress her slowly, savoring the sight of a subtle crimson flush spreading across her ivory collar as I drank her in. I wanted to feel the heat radiating from her breasts as I took each of her nipples in my mouth and teased it against my tongue.

I needed to kiss the slender column of her throat before dipping down and trailing soft kisses across her body until I reached her ankles. She'd circle my neck with her arms, and I'd pick her up and move us to the bed, where I would make love to her gently, slowly, and passionately by rolling all of my lust from our yesteryear into that night—in and out like the tide, flooding us with unstoppable desire. I wouldn't know where I started, and she wouldn't know where she ended. I ached to have that much time with Emma. To show her how much she meant to me.

But fucking Brett.

Anytime I began to pick up the phone and call her or fantasize about the way she'd pumped my dick down her throat, his face would pop up in my mind like a cockblocking ghost I couldn't shake.

"Hello? Son? You there?" My dad reached over to me and thumped my forehead with a flick.

Tripp chuckled beside me.

"Yeah, sorry. What was that?" I asked, tearing my thoughts from my dick hanging from a table and back to the task at hand.

"I was saying … your mom wants us to turn this into something, and before I go on and tell you all what, I need you to agree. So, what will it be?" My dad scuffed his boot across the dirt floor and hooked his thumbs in his pockets, waiting.

"I shot a look at my brothers.

Memphis rolled his tattered sleeves up and let out a grunt. "Yeah, of course I'll help with whatever Mom wants."

"I'm in," Tripp spoke up.

"Aye, me too. Mom deserves what she wants." Sawyer placed his hands on his hips and nodded.

Memphis looked at Sawyer and blew out a breath.

"Let's do it," I agreed.

"Okay. We're going to turn this thing into a wedding venue." My dad opened his hands wide and motioned to the splintering wood, rusted feed buckets, and mud-splattered walls before hanging his head.

"What? Are you kidding me?" Sawyer threw his hands in the air and let them fall to his sides.

"Yuck," Memphis added.

"That doesn't sound so bad!" Tripp clasped his hands under his chin.

I already knew what he was thinking.

"The ranch isn't what it used to be. Money's hard to come by right now. Your mom thinks if we rent this place out, we can bring in some extra income. It's a good idea. I know you boys don't want to make shit pretty. Fine. I'm not asking you to plant flowers or braid each other's hair. I'm asking you to help me clean this place up and get it attractive for guests, which means revenue, which means we aren't struggling. Otherwise, you all need to go get jobs in Weller." My dad kicked the end of his boot on a nearby gate, which was hanging loose on one latch to a stall. The latch broke, and the door crashed to the ground with a puff of dust.

"Sure, Dad." I took a step back and looked around me. "It's got nice bones. Mom's right. It'll make a perfect place to rent. Besides, if there's a wedding, that means there's going to be a lot of jealous bridesmaids looking to dry their tears. They'll be desperate enough to sleep with any of you shitheads."

Only Sawyer responded in excitement, "When can we start?"

"I'm headed to the lumberyard today. Sawyer, come with me. Everyone else, start cleaning it up." My dad turned on his heels and left.

No one spoke until the sound of their horses' muffled hooves faded into the distance.

"You two can get married here. I saw that look in your eyes, Tripp, soon as Dad mentioned wedding. I guess Sawyer and I will be the only eligible Miller bachelors these days since both of you have women. I'll just settle into my role as a silver fox." I strutted around the barn and grabbed a pitchfork. A gnarly splinter pricked my thumb, causing me to drop my tool. It fell to the ground in a clash like cymbals at the end of a drum roll.

"Hell yeah! But Memphis, no. He's going to take that carnie woman and run and join the circus," Tripp jested, shuffling his boots through the scattered straw and kicking it in the air.

Memphis grunted, shaking his head. But he never denied it.

"Tell us about her while Sawyer's gone. I know you two haven't been getting along. But we're still here for you, and we want to know all about her." I dug the splinter from my thumb and shook out my hand before picking up my pitchfork again.

"Here." Tripp pulled a pair of work gloves from his back pocket and tossed them to me.

"She and I aren't a thing. Nor will we ever be. We might look like we match, but we're about as opposite as they come. She's all sunshine, and I'm ..." Memphis threaded a hand through his hair and looked away.

"A grump! Aha!" Tripp pointed a finger in the air and laughed. "Josie told me all about this romance trope! It's real. Oh my gosh! I can't wait to tell her it's true!"

Memphis rolled up his sleeves and clenched his jaw. "I'm not a grump. I just don't subscribe to her line of thinking. And, well ... don't tell Dad, but I've been earning extra money, working gigs at the fairs with her. Course, I couldn't work at that one, considering you goofuses were there. That's part of the reason you saw us arguing."

"There was more than arguing going on between you two, brother. I could have sliced that sexual tension with a dull butter knife."

"We aren't lovers or even friends. We both annoy the shit out of each other. Whatever you saw, just forget it. That's enough rooting around in my business. How about your business and why, after you stayed the night at Emma Jean's, I ain't seen her around here and you haven't left the ranch? You're usually all over the place, bringing women home left and right." Memphis picked up a shovel and paused, awaiting my answer.

"Damn, we live too close together. I can't do shit without one of y'all knowing. Besides, how did you know I was at Emma's? I could have been anywhere," I said.

Tripp whistled nonchalantly, busying himself with a dusty stack of stones in a corner.

"Tripp!" I stabbed my pitchfork in the ground and leaned on it, staring at him until he couldn't ignore me.

"I didn't say anything other than you brought Emma Jean home." Tripp threw his hands in the air and shrank back, a victim of my glare.

Waylan growled at a nearby varmint, scurrying through a heap of sawdust.

I drew in a deep breath and slowly let it out, exchanging glances between my two brothers, who waited patiently for me to explain.

"I stayed at Emma's." The corner of my mouth twitched in a grin I couldn't hide.

"All right!" Tripp swished his hand back and forth out in front of him while thrusting his hips.

Memphis shook his head. " 'Bout time."

"I can neither confirm nor deny what happened that night." I scraped my pitchfork across a stall, scooping up a mixture of old straw and horse manure before carrying it to a pile by the doorway.

"Must not have been special if she ain't hanging around here or you ain't hanging around there," Memphis muttered.

"My night with Emma was absolutely mind-blowing. But I learned some things while I was there." I pressed my lips together, tasting the salty sweat on my upper lip before deciding to continue. "I had a bit of Miller luck."

Tripp sucked in his breath and made the sign of the cross. "I knew it. That storm brought in something bad. It's still not gone either. A little bit of it lingers behind. It brought bad news, didn't it?"

"When you say Miller luck, do you mean, your pecker wouldn't grow? Because you are thirty-something now. You can ask Dad about it. I think that's normal," Memphis called over his shoulder as he brought a scoop of shit to the pile.

"Trust me, my anaconda still bites. Hard," I grunted, continuing shoveling. "But Tripp knows what I'm talking about. I did get some bad news. I wish I could share it, but it's one of those secrets that would do more harm than good if I let it out. So, I carry it. I think … to protect her," I added.

"Don't be so hard on yourself. I got a secret like that, too, for our brother Cole." Tripp tipped his face to the ceiling and whispered something I couldn't hear.

The hair on the back of my neck stood on end. Memphis stopped what he was doing and stared outside the open doors.

"I have one too." Memphis's voice came out low and weighted.

I knew whatever he was thinking about was the cause of that vacant, pained look I always recognized in his eyes.

He cleared his throat and returned to his familiar, relaxed manner. "It'll wear you down. But it goes to the grave with me. I made that decision a long time ago, and it's helped. No more wondering about what-ifs."

"Yep. Same," Tripp agreed, picking up a shovel and getting to work.

"So, you're saying, I should forget what I learned and move on as if I didn't know? Just keep on living with this information?" I asked.

"That's the Miller way. We take the luck of the draw and cope." Memphis tipped his chin up at the clover—our family's symbol—etched above the doorframe.

"Doesn't mean you have to wallow in self-pity. Don't be like me and put your life on hold for years. I say, whatever is bothering you, go outside and whisper it to the sky. Or Scooby. Get it out to ears that can't repeat. Then, give Emma a call and take her on a proper date. You can't let bad news consume you, brother. I should know." Tripp stopped working and studied my face.

I couldn't argue with his wisdom. He'd grown more in the last few months than I had in my entire life. Though Cole's death had rocked our whole family, Tripp's loss of his twin brother had cost him years of anxiety and depression. It wasn't until Josie had come along that our entire family could breathe a sigh of relief, knowing we wouldn't lose him too.

"Thanks. Both of you. I've been going back and forth on if I should mention it to her or not, leaning toward not. It's for the greater good. The only thing it would do is spread more bad news in this world. And this is bad news that doesn't *have* to be shared. What's done is over and ended. I can't hurt her like that." I leaned the pitchfork against the peeling, oak-stained wall and brushed my dirty hands down my jeans.

"Now that you girls got your heart-to-heart out of the way, are we going to clean this shithole up, so we can bang some lonely bridesmaids or what?" Memphis snagged a clump of horsehair from a rusted nail, opened his palm wide, and let it fall to the floor.

"For the lonely bridesmaids!" Tripp roared and thrust his shovel in the air, giving a horrible Viking imitation.

"The last one to clean out a stall is a Madam Von Himperpoot rotten egg!" I shouted.

"A what?" Memphis asked.

"Never mind." I gave him a dismissive wave. "Let's just get to work. I got a woman to apologize to tonight, and I can't smell like a damn barnyard." I sniffed my armpit and winced.

I worked the rest of the day on mentally putting that rat bastard Brett to rest so that the living could move on with the lives they deserved—myself included.

IT WAS JUST after eight p.m. when I trudged home atop a very tired Scooby. After work, he galloped at a slow pace, heading straight into our barn without my guidance.

My brothers had led their horses to the stables long ago, rushing off to their women. I had planned on rushing off to Emma Jean's, but after Tripp had received a very excited call from Josie, they'd both told me to hold off one more night. They had something up their sleeve. I wasn't going to argue with anyone who could help me in the dating department. My track record with women was dismal and could be summed up in one phrase—*open mouth and insert foot.*

I did that a lot. Once, I'd stupidly told a semi-steady girl-friend that I was going through a weird spell. It was years ago during a really trying time on the ranch. My johnson wouldn't get hard for shit. I tried everything to get my libido going, but no matter what kind of wacky root or vitamin I took, my dick stopped working. My girlfriend worried I was losing interest in her and immediately began to panic. But I didn't have the balls to tell her that it was all me and maybe I was just growing old.

Instead, I told her that even the hot chicks at the gym weren't getting me hard. Which was the damn truth, but I delivered it all wrong. What I'd meant to say was just that— but not. I had meant to make her feel better, but instead, I'd stuck my foot in my mouth and made her feel worse.

It wasn't long after that she had begun accompanying me to the gym, and after three sessions, she'd left me for a hulking gym rat who could probably break her in half with his hard rama-lama-ding-dong. I couldn't blame her. It wasn't the first time I'd run my mouth before my brain could catch up. The problem was, my brain was usually stuck in my other head—the one that hadn't been working at the time.

If I had a real shot with Emma, after I'd just upped and left her after the most amazing sex, I needed a full-on support system. Who knew what she had in store for me after the way I'd left? She scared me just as much as her ferocious mama did. One snap of her eyes to mine, and I felt like a whip had lashed across my cheeks. Just being next to her mom sometimes made my balloon knot squeeze so tight that I could mold a diamond.

I knew I was in for an ass-chewing when the time came. So, naturally, like any other man, I avoided it for another day. Besides, whatever Josie and Tripp had planned would certainly work better than what I had planned—a groveling apology and maybe a hint at another round or two on her massage table. And although that was an offer I would jump on, I didn't think Emma Jean would take the bait. I would end up putting my foot in my mouth, as always.

"Scooby, she's going to run off again into the sunset. I just know it." I put my arms around my horse and rested my head next to his before closing him in his stable. "I fucked it up."

Scooby whinnied.

I filled his feed bucket and gave him fresh water before turning off the lights and telling the rest of the horses good night. They were as close to me as my brothers, sometimes even more so.

I'd told Scooby about Brett and Emma the morning I left her. I whispered it into his ears so that I could get the words out of my chest. They were eating me alive, choking me from the inside out. And my horse knew it. He'd been jittery ever since the storm.

"Good night, boys. We ride again tomorrow!" I said, stepping outside and locking the barn doors.

The lights in my parents' house switched on, but I didn't have the energy or the heart to pay a visit. Buffy was calling my name, and so was my hand as thoughts of Emma Jean and her milking table pummeled my weak resistance.

My phone vibrated in my back pocket.

"Shit. What now?" I said to myself, pulling it out and checking the name.

Tripp.

"Change of plans. Go shower and meet me at my place in thirty minutes. You want a shot with your high school sweetheart, you're going to need to sing like a bird," Tripp said as soon as I answered.

"What? You mean, tell her my secrets?" I asked, stopping in my tracks. My heart plummeted deep into my belly, and my balls shriveled into hiding.

"No! I mean, really *sing*. Tonight's karaoke night at Bushwacker. Emma, Josie, and even Abilene will be there. You can prove your worthiness in front of all of Buck Off. Except, well, Mama Sue. Good luck winning that old lady over."

"Both Emma and her mom are going to be at the bar?"

"Yes."

"And you want me to sing to them?" I threw my hand in the air, on the verge of panic. This wasn't the plan I'd hoped for. A grovel and nudge toward her massage table was looking more and more like the easier way out.

"To Emma."

"Who the hell had this bright idea? Have you ever heard me sing? I sound like a horny moose, looking for a mate."

"I'd describe it as more of a drowning beaver."

"Beavers can drown?" My attention bounced from wildlife to my pathetic current predicament.

"Damn it. Meet me at my place in thirty minutes. Hurry. I've convinced Sawyer and Memphis to come too. Although they refuse to sing," he said.

"Wait. We're all going out? All of the brothers? Together?" I asked.

This had to be some kind of joke. My brothers and I hadn't enjoyed a night out together since Sawyer had graduated high school.

"I told them she's your Josie and that Emma Jean is going to run again if we don't get to her for you," he said.

I sucked in a breath.

"And guess what." I could hear a smile in his voice.

"What?" I asked.

"They said, family's family."

I wiped my palm across my unshaven jaw and swallowed hard.

"Family's family." I nodded. As I dangled on the edge of emotion, my voice squeaked out, "Thanks, Tripp."

I hung up the phone and hightailed it to my cabin, singing, "*Do, re, me, fa, sol, la, ti, do*," to warm up my vocals and my heart for what would come next.

CHAPTER ELEVEN

EMMA

I SWUNG OPEN THE DOORS TO THE SALOON JUST AS THE PLACE grew crowded. I always knew how to make an entrance. If I waited a half hour after the typical time everyone rushed into the bar, when I strutted inside, all eyes would fall on me. Usually, in Gillibrook, that was a bad thing. But tonight, I had my mama and my best friend by my side. No turd muffin, nincompoop, or gossiping toad could derail me from having a good time.

I placed one high heel in front of the other and sashayed my way through the narrow paths between tables, motioning for my mom and Josie to follow me to the far end of the center bar. Dozens of acquaintances from my past sat, slumped in their chairs, mouth-breathing and staring, wide-eyed, as my entourage passed. My mother hadn't graced the saloon since my dad had left, and I hadn't graced it since I'd left years ago. Josie, on the other hand, had apparently become a regular.

"Howdy there, Kenneth! How about a round of whiskeys

for my ladies and me?" Josie set her clutch on the bar and grabbed the stool facing the door. "I sat here on my first date with Tripp. It's a lucky stool. He got shot in the ass that night with a rogue dart, but still, it was a lucky night," she assured us.

"Sure thing, Josie. Whiskies coming right up." Kenneth, the bartender, threw a dishrag over his shoulder and grabbed a handful of glasses.

I dropped down next to Josie and hung my purse on a hook tucked underneath the counter. My mom settled in beside me, following my lead. I could feel the room's breath on my neck.

I wanted to turn around and shout at them, *What are you looking at?* But later, I'd let my flawless rendition of "Bad Reputation" by Joan Jett do the talking for me.

"You okay?" my mom asked, scooting the metal barstool legs across the concrete floor and closer to me.

"Yeah, I'm fine. I just … I've dated quite a few of these knuckleheads in here." I turned my attention away from my past mistakes and toward a group at a corner table on the other side of the room.

A beautiful woman with blonde-and-black-streaked hair and a redheaded lady wearing a garnet choker across her slender neck sat with their backs flush against the booth. They chatted and laughed with three devilishly handsome men across from them. The men looked like brothers, all massively tall with inky-black hair that fell into their eyes. One of the brothers scanned the room underneath a wide-brimmed cowboy hat. When his eyes met mine, my heart lurched inside my chest.

"They aren't from around here," I whispered to my mom and Josie, unable to tear my gaze from his.

"Nope." Kenneth set three glasses of whiskey in front of us and lowered his voice, leaning across the counter. "They came through the night we had that big storm right as the power went out. They own a winery down in someplace called Morningwood. I guess they're traveling around to find purchasers or something. I couldn't afford to buy more than one case though. Damn shit was expensive. You'd think it was some type of miraculous drug for the price they were asking for it. Anyway, I bought a case because they gave me the heebie-jeebies and I thought they'd leave. But they're sticking around for some reason or another."

"Interesting. Something about that blonde-and-black-haired lady looks familiar, but I can't put my finger on it." Josie reached for a glass and brought it to her lips, tossing back her drink as easy as if it were water.

"Anyway, let's toast to a girls' night before Brother Roger gets here." My mom reached for her glass and held it up, rattling the ice against the bottom and dribbling amber liquid down the side.

I grabbed my drink and gently bumped it against theirs.

"To ... tonight," I said, unable to yet truly allow myself the opportunity to believe I was staying or that I was sitting next to my mom in a bar.

I'd sat next to her at church, a funeral, a movie, and at any of my fair competitions once I left the stage. But I'd never sat next to my mom out and about at a bar. Even Mama Sue had snapped a photo of us before we left and made us promise to "come back with one hell of a story or don't come back at all."

"To tonight!" Mom and Josie echoed.

"Wait. So, I get to meet His Holy Hotness?" Josie asked. Her glass was already nearly half-empty, and we were just getting started.

"Holy Hotness? Really?" Abilene shook her head, bouncing her curls over her shoulders. They flowed down her back, same as mine.

I never understood why my beautiful mother wanted to stay in Gillibrook with the riffraff when she could have had the world in the palm of her hand. She'd kept herself up, like all of us Presley women do, through hard work and Botox. Hell, half the men in here weren't staring in my direction. They were not so subtly drooling over her.

I threw my drink back in one big gulp and smoothed out the end of my miniskirt while eyeing the stage. I'd always shone in the limelight. To see and be seen was the story of my life—besides the whole *hold 'em and fold 'em* thing … with much more folding 'em. But this town had squashed my passion for entertaining and run me right out of here. And now, here I sat, staring at the men and women who'd paved that treacherous path.

"Why, look what the cougar dragged in." A man's voice slithered in my ear. His breath smelled of stale cigarettes and cheap beer.

I turned in my seat and faced Marshall, a man I'd dated years ago before dropping him like a bad habit. On our second date, he'd told me how crazy all of his ex-girlfriends were, which was an obvious red flag that meant *he* was the crazy one. I had enough crazy at home. I didn't want to date it. I quickly broke things off and moved on. Or so I thought. He blew up my phone for two straight weeks, begging for another chance. After too many creepy texts and voice mails, I'd finally blocked his number.

"Oh, hey." I leaned back from the stream of his hot breath and tucked a strand of hair behind my ear.

Beside me, Josie scrunched her nose. I side-eyed my mom's reaction, but she kept a straight face, observing the situation.

"You know, I called you so many times. What happened? Did you change your number?" he slurred, dribbling a string of drool down the side of his mouth and wiping it with the back of his hand.

"I told you, things weren't going to work out. That's what happened," I said, straightening my spine to my full height and lengthening myself on the barstool.

"Well, why the hell not? What's wrong with me?" He hiccuped, swaying on the back of his heels and stumbling backward.

The handsome visitor with the cowboy hat popped up beside Marshall and grabbed him by the collar, growling, "Besides the obvious?" A row of gleaming white teeth peeked out from his snarling upper lip.

His brothers gathered behind him.

I didn't know if I wanted to run or jump in the middle. But one glance at Josie, and I knew what she was thinking. Her eyes met mine, fell to the sexy men's groins, and back up to me with a nod. She mouthed a word I couldn't quite make out.

E-verse hair 'em?

Nurse spare 'em?

Traverse scare 'em?

"Oh good! Look who just walked through the door! Brother Roger is here!" My mom cut in, motioning for Brother Roger to come forward.

The tourists' eyes flew open as the preacher strolled toward us.

"Leave her alone. I can tell you're up to no good. I smell it on you." The cowboy uncurled his fist from Marshall's collar and shoved him aside. "I'm watching you," he told Marshall before he swiftly left, heading back to his seat with his brothers following closely behind him.

"Holy shit!" Josie blurted before jerking her eyes toward Brother Roger and wincing. "Sorry! So sorry, Father! That's a sin. That. Is. A. Sin!" She giggled into her empty glass and hid her red face before whispering into my ear, "And so were my thoughts about all those sexy guys taking up for you. That was something straight out of a movie! You could reverse-harem 'em or, you know, reverse-cowgirl 'em. Or both."

"You're okay." Brother Roger waved Josie's concern away and offered his hand, introducing himself. "I'm Roger, *and* I'm off the clock. Besides, I didn't hear anything." He settled on the barstool beside my mom and winked at me.

"Glad you could make it," I told him sincerely.

As soon as he'd walked through the door, my mom had been sporting the same contagious goofy grin that was contaminating our water these days. Josie had it, Tripp had it, my mom and Brother Roger had it. I even noticed it on damn near half of the folks inside the bar.

"I am too. It's not often I get to come to the, uh … saloon." He tugged his shirt collar.

"It's not often I get to see my mom have a good time. So, thank you for coming out for her." I held up my hand for another whiskey and winked at my mom.

"Oh, Emma Jean. You can be sweet when you wanna." My mom put her arm around me and hugged my shoulders before turning back to Brother Roger.

It was the first hug we'd shared since I'd been home. We had a long way to go.

"Hey! Psst. Back to that hot piece of ass over there, defending you." Josie squeezed my knee.

"May I have your attention, please?" Marshall's voice slurred over the microphone. "We have a special guest with us tonight. Her name's Emma Jean. But you all might know her as the county fair pageant queen from years and years and years and years and years ago. Ain't that right, honey? How old are yer now?"

"Shit," I muttered, swiveling my barstool around to face the stage head-on.

Josie pulled out her phone and started to text.

The crowd grew silent, exchanging nervous glances between Marshall and me.

"I want to serenade this sweet lady who broke my heart. You see, she dumped me after two … two …" He held up three fingers. "Anyway, here we go!"

Marshall pushed a few buttons on the karaoke machine and somehow managed to start the music. The brothers from earlier moved toward the stage, circling his performance. Marshall began to squeak out a nerve-rattling rendition of "Achy Breaky Heart." The saloon cringed.

I drank my entire glass of whiskey, the liquid courage calming my nerves and filtering through my brain as I thought of what kind of comeback I could make after this fiasco. But as the music and that douche-bag Marshall quieted, my night kept getting worse. I'd vowed to have a good time, but little by little, my big night out was spiraling out of control.

"Let's go, honey. Come on. Get up. We're going to sing 'These Boots Are Made for Walkin'.' " My mom tugged my hand, yanking me to my feet.

"Anyone have any more requests?" Marshall blew me a kiss.

The room erupted in whispers.

"I think we've heard enough of that awful voice of yours. How about you come off the stage and rest?" the cowboy from earlier said above the whispers.

"I'll sing with you." Josie abruptly stood up. "I'll sing a big ol' fuck you!" She pointed to Marshall and quickly gasped, remembering Brother Roger. "Sorry, Reverend," she called over her shoulder. "Again."

"Shit. Shit. Shit. That escalated quickly." I snatched my wrist from my mom and shook my head. "I got this." I threw my arms out wide. "Wow! It looks like the whole male population in Gillibrook has little-dick syndrome tonight. Got anything else you'd like to throw at me while you're at it?"

A few women in the room clapped.

"I do! I got a request! You dumped me, too, after one date!" someone shouted from the crowd. "How about 'Cold As Ice'?"

"Aye! And me after four dates!" said another voice. "Play 'Killer Queen'!"

Crap. This isn't good.

I swallowed hard but kept my head held high. Beside me, my mother's face grew madder than a hornet. She stiffened, setting her chin in defiance, like a warrior waiting on me to give her the command to ride into battle. The air grew stifling, squeezing any last effort I had to fight right out of me.

"Let's give it a rest! That's enough!" Kenneth shouted before tapping me on my shoulder and handing me a double. "It's on me."

I gladly accepted it and began to drink.

"How about 'You Give Love a Bad Name'? She dumped me by text after we dated a month! Beat that!" A burly man stood up.

I didn't even recognize him.

" 'Maneater'!" someone shouted.

"If any of you were worth dating my daughter, I might agree with you. I'm hard on her too. But all I see is a bunch of out-of-shape mouth-breathers who couldn't even finish high school. She's miles above and beyond you pitiful lot."

Brother Roger sucked in his breath, fanning himself.

I curled my fingers into my palm, digging my nails into my skin to keep from collapsing in a heap of embarrassment. The heat radiating off my cheeks drifted to my eyes, burning them from the inside out. The silence inside the saloon grew deafening until the swinging doors flew open, banging against the walls, and all four Miller brothers sauntered inside.

"I heard we have a bunch of knuckleheads in here who think Gillibrook's pageant queen owes them something," West said, dragging his boots across the floor toward me. He towered over the crowd, his footsteps echoing in the nearly silent room.

Josie looked at me and nodded to her phone on the counter. *I had to*, she mouthed, shrugging.

Marshall shrank onstage, snapping his eyes back and forth between the out-of-town brothers in front of him and the Miller brothers coming toward him.

West pointed at one of the men seated on his right as he passed, but he didn't stop walking or even pause. "Curly, Emma Jean dumped you because your teeth are as yellow as summer corn baking in the Gillibrook sun. You need to brush your teeth! I ain't ever smelled a cooked dog turd, but I can imagine it's what your breath smells like."

He kept leisurely strolling forward, calling out every douche bag I'd ever dated. Sawyer, Tripp, and even Memphis slowly followed behind West, cracking their knuckles and casting menacing glances toward the stage.

"John, she dumped you because you're forty-two and you live with your mama, who still washes your clothes and cooks you three meals a day. You told me so yourself! That ain't attractive, man."

He continued, "Luke, she dumped you because you have a kid showing up seems about every year and calling you daddy."

A chorus of giggles echoed around the room.

"You got that right! You owe me child support, you bastard!" a woman shouted.

The woman with black streaks in her hair stepped onstage. "Give me this." She snatched the microphone from

Marshall, brought it to her lips, and softly spoke with a voice that was like a calming melody straight out of a fairy tale. "And she dumped you because you look like a bowl of grundle butter baked inside a molded pumpkin. Now, get out of here." She kicked him in the leg, sending him tumbling offstage, landing on his ass.

"What's grundle butter?" Josie whispered beside me.

I couldn't answer. I was too focused on standing upright.

"I've had enough of these assholes. How about you all?" the woman cooed into the microphone. She wore a pair of yellow diamond earrings in the shape of sunflowers. Something about the way she moved and the way she talked instantly charmed the room and set the diners at ease.

The crowd mumbled, nodding in agreement.

"You okay?" West whispered as he paused next to me, throwing his arms around me and clutching my body to his to stop my trembles.

"Take me out of here," I whispered back, unable to meet his eyes.

For once in my life, my poker face had slipped so far down that it circled my ankles like an oversize pair of granny panties. I couldn't move.

He nodded, grabbed my hand, and whisked me away, dragging me out in his firm grip, like I glided on air. My mom, Josie, and the rest of our group followed us out in silence.

"Seems like the lot of them get butt hurt when a pretty woman turns them down. I'm new in town, but this place could use a little more peace and a lot less … *shit*," the woman continued.

The crowd cheered.

"One, two, three. One, two, three, three. Hit it!" I heard the woman shout before we exited the bar, slamming the door shut behind us.

In the background, she began to sing "I Put a Spell on You."

"Honey, let's go back in there and show them what you're made of. I'll be right beside you. We can still win this," my mother said, urging me to turn around, her eyes brimming with tears. She was just as humiliated as I was.

The rest of our group lagged behind, busying themselves with recounts of what had just happened.

"No. I don't want to win this one, Mom. I made my bed. Now, I'm lying in it. I'll be fine. You all go on home. I need to speak to West." I shooed my mother away. "Really, I'm okay. Promise."

"Don't be out too late. I'll be worried sick, and so will Mama Sue. If you decide not to come home ... text me at least, please." She patted my hand and turned to leave.

"And, Emma?" She turned back, her voice filled with desperation. "Please don't go. I'm real proud of how you held your head high in there. Those assholes didn't know what hit them." She made finger guns in the air and playfully shot them off before returning to Brother Roger, who stood, waiting in the shadows.

Josie jogged up to me and embraced me in a surprisingly forceful hug. "You sure you don't want me to beat the shit out of them?" she asked.

"No. It's fine. Besides, I think West shut them up for a while," I said.

"Yeah, about that. I had plans for the brothers to meet us tonight. They were already on their way here. It was a teeny-tiny surprise for karaoke night. But at the first sign of trouble, I contacted Tripp to tell them all to hurry it up. He'd been telling me about this dark feeling he had, and, well, I trust his intuition. So, I told him. Good thing I did! Once we got out of there, he said he was feeling a bit better. Like a veil is lifting or something. I don't understand it, but …" She shrugged.

"Well, thank you for looking out for me. And for coming out with me tonight. I'm sorry it didn't turn into a raging party-fest and that your surprise—or shall I say, match-making shenanigans—was ruined. But there's always Weller or another crawfish boil."

"Count me in!" Her lips split into a wide grin as she bounced away.

When everyone left, West led me to his truck and opened the tailgate.

"Upsy-daisy. Let's chat." He picked me up, propped me on the gate, and lifted himself to sit beside me. "Are you okay? What was all that about? And why were you partying with your mom? I've never seen Abilene at such a place."

"I'm fine. And my mom and I are … *working* on things." I wrung my hands in my lap. My skirt wrinkled across my thighs, streaked with dirt from his truck.

"Good. Does that mean you're staying? Because then maybe I don't have to sing the damn song Josie was pushing me to do for karaoke night," he said, wiping a hand across his forehead in dramatics.

I snapped my eyes to his and noticed for the first time that the goofy grin he carried matched his brothers'.

An unfamiliar flutter sparked in my belly.

"Wait. You were going to sing for me?" I asked.

"Uh, no." He laughed. "But I told Josie I would. I was just hoping it wouldn't get to that point. I planned on winning you over before then."

"Win me over? You barely spoke to me after I milked your wanker under my massage table. And now, you want to come crawling back into my good graces?" I looked down my nose at him, rolled my eyes, and blew out a breath. "And you call me the Heartbreak Queen."

"It's not like that. I couldn't ... I just ... I had some stuff to take care of. I needed to clear my head after what happened and sort my feelings. I'm sorry."

"What feelings? Feelings of guilt for that night? Loving and leaving? It's fine. I do it all the time." I turned my face away.

"Damn it, you're as stubborn as a constipated mule. My feelings, Emma. Mine." He slid his hand under my chin and gently forced my gaze in his direction. "What happened the other night was something I'd wanted to happen since we were teenagers. Do you have any idea how much I think about you? Still? I joke about you breaking hearts because I'm a jealous son of a bitch. Just like all those dumbasses in there." He cast a ruthless glance back at the bar. "They're jealous they can't have you."

The singer's voice carried outside. She sang a hypnotizing melody that put even my fragile state at ease.

"I thought you were still mad at me for Kyle," I said as he inched closer to me, brushing his thumb across my trembling lip. A burst of heat curled up my spine, escaping my mouth in a soft sigh.

"No. I've never been mad. Jealous, yes. I was like them in there. I wanted to know why and what was wrong with me. I didn't stop to think it wasn't about me." He hesitated. "It was about you and all the shit you'd been through with your mom and dad."

I held my breath, unsure if I wanted to fall into his arms or push him away—or both.

"Look, I understand now. I needed to get to you to explain that and say I was sorry for all the past drama. But the past is the past. I don't live that way anymore. I live in the here and now." He dropped his hands and rubbed them down his blue jeans.

"Oh yeah?" I asked. "It's that easy?"

"Hell no, it ain't easy. But I don't want to be stuck. And that's how you get stuck. I might not want big-city life and fancy-schmancy corporate shit like you. But I do want more. I want to live. And that's why I'm here tonight. I think you should live a little here too. I want to show you how. I want to give you a chance." His voice trailed off as he jumped off of the truck and stood in front of me, grasping my knees and forcing them apart to step closer.

"You've been running a long time. Let me carry you. We can cross the finish line together. All those events we competed in don't mean a thing. I didn't want to win over you. I wanted to win you." He took off his cowboy hat and tossed it into the bed of his truck before pressing his forehead to mine. "You're the blue ribbon, Emma Jean. And they all know it in there. There's no one in this town good enough for you, and that makes them all upset. Myself included."

I shrank back from him and rubbed my chest. It felt like he had shot a hole the size of Texas right through it.

"What song were you going to sing for me?" I asked, barely able to keep my voice straight.

" 'Stay' by Maurice Williams and the Zodiacs. You know, the one in *Dirty Dancing*? Josie told me it was your favorite movie. I wasn't sure if I should dance with you or sing to you. You're liable to keep running if I do either." He leaned forward, grasping my hands in his and pulling me back up straight, inches from his face.

"Don't do either then."

"That's not an option. I—" he started.

I yanked him to me, smothered his words with my lips, and brushed my mouth against his. The lady inside had quit singing, and the only sounds outside of the saloon were a chorus of crickets and the erratic thumping of our hearts, beating down their walls.

He opened his mouth and asked, "Does this mean you won't go?" His lips were still crushed against mine.

I pulled back and laughed, not bothering to tell him I'd already planned on staying a little longer anyway. His persistence and prize-worthy speech were refreshing to hear regardless. Some things were better kept to myself in the here and now, just like he'd said.

"It means, I'm staying *for now*. But I need to take things slow. You okay with that?" I asked, hooking my legs around his waist.

His metal belt buckle dug in hard between my thighs as he pressed himself against me.

"I've waited over a decade for you. What's a little longer going to hurt?" He flashed me a goofy grin.

I reached behind me, grabbed his cowboy hat, and set it atop my head, mirroring his expression.

My mama had taught me not to break for any man. But for West Miller, I could at least learn to bend. After all, slow and steady won the race, and I was always up for a challenge.

EPILOGUE

EMMA JEAN

SIX MONTHS LATER

"So, let me get this straight. You finally got the nerve to set foot back in Bushwacker, and Kenneth had no idea what you were talking about?" Josie plucked a dandelion from the grass and blew on it, scattering its seeds in the gusty wind.

"I'm telling you, it's like he plumb forgot my utter humiliation! Weirdest thing. But I've decided to leave it. Besides, no sense in living in the past." I lay down on my back and stared up at the clouds gathering overhead. The sun had dipped below Mount Odina, casting a warm glow over the valley.

Josie and I had been sitting outside all day, planning her upcoming wedding. She'd piled magazines, articles, and books on our picnic blanket while we drank champagne and hashed out details.

"It doesn't surprise me. Tripp's told me some stories

about this town that I can't wrap my head around. I've done a bit of digging in the library too. Found some old, archaic newspaper clippings about all sorts of things. Like people vanishing into thin air. But that stuff doesn't bother me. I kind of like it here. Gillibrook's got character." She flopped onto her back and stared up at the sky with me.

"Yeah, it's growing on me too. Never thought I'd say that." I draped my arm across my eyes and sighed.

"You're growing. That's why," she said. I could detect a smile in her voice without even looking at her.

"I was forced to grow when I had nowhere to go. It was a blessing in disguise, I suppose."

"You're damn right it was. Was last night the first time you ever told a man you loved him?" She rolled over onto her belly and grabbed another magazine, flipping through it.

"Last night was the first time a man ever told me he loved me. I'd told Tommy once. He pretended like he hadn't heard me. I never said it again." A sudden chill filled the early spring air as I forced the thought of my past out of my way.

"His loss. You got a good one now. We might even be sisters-in-law one day!" Her face lit up, still sporting a goofy grin.

"No rush!" I threw my hands in the air, opening my palms like she held me up at gunpoint. "He knows I'm taking it slow. But, yeah, maybe one day."

Memphis's motorcycle revved in the background, drawing our attention toward him. A woman with long hair peeking out from underneath her helmet clung to his back. Beaded crystal jewels hung from her wrists, catching the light.

"Who is that?" I bolted upright.

"Oh, you haven't heard? Memphis is working for the carnies now. I think that might be his boss or something. I'm not sure. Tripp only mentioned it in passing. I had a sense he was trying to keep his brother's secret, so I didn't want to be nosy." Josie propped herself up on her elbow.

Memphis and the woman parked outside his cabin, followed by a plume of dust from the gravel they'd kicked up. The lady slipped off the back of the motorcycle and pulled her helmet from her head, shaking out her hair. I could spot her ruby-red lipstick from down the road.

"She's definitely not from Gillibrook," I said, studying their movements.

I didn't know much about Memphis other than what West had told me. Memphis had always been the quiet type, preferring solitude to camaraderie. He rebelled against their ranch as the black sheep of the family. When West mentioned his brother's struggles, I thought Memphis and I had a lot in common. If I could learn to love our quirky hometown, then he could too. But the way he looked at the woman in front of him told me otherwise. He was one suitcase short of hightailing it out of here with her in the driver's seat.

"Nope. Definitely not." Josie hummed the "Wedding March." "Maybe she can catch my bouquet since … you know, you're taking things *slow*."

"I know when to hold 'em, and I know when to fold 'em. I play my cards right. That's all. Sometimes, the game lasts longer that way, but that's how I make sure I win."

I glanced over my shoulder at her, but she hid her face, tucked between the pages of a magazine.

"You think your mom is folding 'em with Brother Roger? Can you imagine your new daddy being a preacher man?" She peeked over the pages and adjusted her glasses.

"I think my mom's finally growing up too. She hasn't even bad-mouthed my dad in months. All she talks about is Brother Roger." I sighed. "I can see the change in her though. It's refreshing but also a little scary."

"Sounds like the same change I see in you."

"Like mother, like daughter." I pressed my fingertips to my collar, smoothing down the laced edges that Mama Sue had sewn on last week.

She'd been practicing her skills for next season's sewing competition at the county fair after one of her ex-friends won it last time. She'd never forgiven those old broads for whatever they'd done to her. I had a feeling my grandma had just as much baggage to unpack as both my mama and me. But she would take her stubbornness to the grave. Mama Sue was the champion matriarch, and the fierce Presley legend was her ultimate game. No matter if she still crumbled at my grandfather's voice recording.

The sound of hooves stomping across dirt echoed across the pasture, tearing my thoughts from Buck Off's legendary reputation.

West, Tripp, and Sawyer galloped into view, steering a group of cattle toward the barn in the distance. The brothers dashed through the pasture, swerving on their horses and sitting up in their saddles. West rode in the front, leading his brothers home.

"There they are!" I flashed a grin without bothering to wipe it from my face. Just because I was hell-bent on taking my new relationship slow didn't mean I couldn't fall into line like I'd fallen into love—unapologetically. I'd spent enough of my life avoiding feeling.

Whether there really was something in the water in Gillibrook or if West Miller was just the perfect man to coax these butterflies out of me, I sank into the comfort of knowing I could stay and still be a winner. Because living life with newfound hope and family—blood-related or not—had proven to be the ultimate prize.

Thank you for reading Emma Jean and West's story! Are you

ready to keep on riding with the Miller brothers? Check out *WANTED: Sunny Caster, Sweet Disaster* and continue the Buck Off series today!

Sign up for my NEWSLETTER to find out my latest releases and claim your free, exclusive e-book!

Join my Facebook group, DTF (Dirty. Tough. Females.), for sneak peeks, shenanigans, and more!

ALSO BY KAT ADDAMS

Dirty South Series

Faking Second Chances

Schooling Professor Playboy

Playing Backstage with the Rockstar

Stroking the Boss's ... Ego

Mayday (FREE for Newsletter Subscribers)

DTF (Dirty. Tough. Female.) Series

On the Rox

Cream-Pied

Whip it Out

Just the Tip

FU (FORKS UNIVERSITY FASHION ACADEMY) SERIES

Just Between Us

This Means War

BUCK OFF RANCH SERIES

Josie Thatcher, Cowboy Catcher

Emma Jean, Heartbreak Queen

Sunny Caster, Sweet Disaster

PARANORMAL ROMANTIC COMEDY

Ghosted

WRITING PARANORMAL ROMANTIC COMEDY AS FRITZI COX

For a complete listing of Kat Addams books, visit

https://kataddams.com

ACKNOWLEDGMENTS

As always, thank you to my little girl for being my biggest fan even if you have no idea what I'm writing. You are the most important person in my life and forever will be. I'll try not to be overbearing like Abilene, but once that first boy breaks your heart, all bets are off. Mama tried.

Thank you to my editor, Jovana Shirley; my cover designer, Lori Jackson; my graphics designer, Kat Lopez; and Ashley Blank, the best assistant I could ask for. I am so damn lucky to have such an amazing team of women working with me to pull these stories together.

Thank you to my mom, who I still butt heads with all the time. I know you are only trying to protect me. I love you. Family is family even if we are both as stubborn as constipated mules.

And lastly, thank you to my man, Dustin—or as I like to call him, The D. You took a wrecking ball to my walls, and I am forever grateful. You will always be my blue ribbon.

ABOUT THE AUTHOR

Kat Addams is an author of contemporary romantic comedies. She's had a passion for making readers laugh since she wrote her first over-the-top comic book at the age of eight, earning her high marks and concerning looks from her grade-school teachers. She's a graduate of the University of Memphis, where she studied English literature and creative writing, and fell in love with the rom-com genre. Her books can be described as equal parts shameless and heartwarming with a heavy dose of heat.

When she's not writing about exotic men and daydreaming of worldly travels, you can find Kat in her hometown of Memphis, drinking craft cocktails on patios and raising her mini-me with a girl-power attitude—but not necessarily in that order. In her downtime, she loves to embark on outdoor adventures, empower other women, and lose herself in good books and good music.

Kat satisfies her darker side by writing paranormal romance with wicked humor under the name Fritzi Cox. Fritzi provides Kat with an outlet to cause mayhem and debauchery with an element of suspense. Whether you're reading a book from either Fritzi or Kat, you're guaranteed a hilarious adventure.